Bringing Home Mr Bacon

Nikki Perry & Kirsty Roby

1st edition, 2024

Edited by Eva Chan

ISBN 978-1-9911972-5-2 (paperback)

ISBN 978-1-9911972-6-9 (Epub)

Cover design and layout by Yummy Book Covers

Typeset in PT Serif, 10pt

To all the Barbaras of the world.

to all the Barbaras of the world.

Never trust a skinny chef.

Acknowledgements

Thank you so much for reading *Bringing Home Mr Bacon*. If you enjoy the book, *please* consider leaving us a review.

If you would like to read more of our work, you can find out about our other books here:
www.nikkiperryandkirstyroby.com

Thank you to Eva Chan for the copy-editing and to Yummy Book Covers for the gorgeous artwork and formatting.

Bringing Home Mr Bacon

Eggplant Kasundi

....

Ingredients:

1/4 cup vegetable oil

1 eggplant, cut into 1.5 cm-thick pieces

1 brown onion, coarsely chopped

2 tsp mustard seeds

1 Tbsp finely chopped fresh ginger

2 long fresh green chillies, seeded and finely chopped

2 cloves garlic, coarsely chopped

1 Tbsp cumin seeds

2 tsp paprika

1/2 tsp turmeric

1 x 400 g can diced tomatoes

1/4 cup of brown sugar

2 Tbsp malt vinegar

Method:

Heat oil in a large saucepan over high heat. Cook half the eggplant, stirring, for 5 minutes or until golden. Use a slotted spoon to transfer to a plate. Repeat with remaining eggplant, reheating the pan between batches.

Reduce the heat to medium.

Cook the onion, stirring often, for 3 minutes or until golden.

Add mustard seeds and cook, stirring, for 2 minutes or until the seeds start to pop.

Add the ginger, chilli and garlic. Cook, stirring, for 1 minute until soft.

Add the cumin, paprika and turmeric and stir to combine.

Add back in the eggplant, then tomato, sugar and vinegar and reduce heat to low.

Simmer, stirring, for 30 minutes or until the mixture thickens. Season with salt and pepper. Set aside to cool slightly.

Tessa

Why did all diet food have to taste so bloody similar to wood shavings? Tessa contemplated as she forced down the last of her Atkins shake. It was only day four and she was already over it. She'd never make it another two weeks, despite her desire to lose enough weight to fit back into her silver dress. Eyeing the passionfruit layer cake on her kitchen counter with a longing akin to a nympho in a nudist camp, she quickly boxed it up before she could cave in and slice off a piece for herself. It was for her ex mother-in-law's birthday and had turned out beautifully. It was close to two o'clock and she had orders to complete, but Keith still hadn't shown up. What's the bet he would turn up right when she was at a crucial point in the cooking process and throw her off?

The aroma of onions and spices simmering for one of her popular chutneys filled the kitchen. She added eggplant to the preserving pan and gave it a stir.

As if she had conjured him, a car door slammed. Tessa

watched with amusement as her ex-husband got out of his mid-life crisis on wheels and attempted to straighten the landscaping sign next to her letterbox before kicking at one of the garden gnomes placed haphazardly along the path. It was the one she secretly thought of as 'Big D' because it vaguely resembled her old high school boyfriend Darren. Big D wobbled but didn't fall over. Keith kicked at the gnome again, mounted the front steps with a slight limp and leant against the doorbell. After a couple of minutes of incessant buzzing, Tessa picked up the cake box, made her way to the door and opened it. Keith pushed past, glaring down at her.

"Where the hell do these fucking garden gnomes keep coming from? You know it's not a good look for my business."

"You're more than welcome to move the signage to your own yard," Tessa told him, "since your business has nothing to do with me any more." She called up the stairs: "Abigail, Dad's here."

"We've been over this," Keith told her, raking a flat palm through his slightly thinning blond hair to give it some depth. "I need an established garden that reflects my landscaping skills, and our place is too small. I've put years of work into that garden, and these bloody gnomes are not the aesthetic I'm after."

Too bad he hadn't put more work into their marriage, Tessa thought, but stayed quiet. The garish gnomes were a bit petty, but an immensely satisfying way of taking back some control over her ex.

"Finally." Abigail emerged from upstairs wearing a short summer dress and pulling her long dark hair up into a messy bun. "You said you'd be here ages ago."

Tessa handed her the cake box. "You look lovely, honey. Give this, and my love, to Nana." She leant in to give her daughter a quick one-sided hug before heading back to work. "Bye, Keith," she called absently over her shoulder.

...

The kitchen was her favourite room in the house. After the break-up, she had remortgaged the house and put in a commercial kitchen, stainless steel and practical with a large double sink and lots of bench space but with a layout that worked for her equally well as a family space. Pride of place was her Italian freestanding oven that she'd chosen over replacing her car for something newer.

Now, she spent all her spare time — when she wasn't working her part-time job — concocting, making, labelling and selling her homemade sauces, chutneys and dressings. It was only a small business, but she was proud of it, and everything she had learnt.

Tessa was sticking labels on kasundi jars when there was a quick knock on her dining room door and it slid open.

"I have wine," Sonya said, waggling a bottle of rosé in one hand as she emerged, resplendent in a hibiscus-patterned mumu. "I saw Keith Jerky leaving and figured you might need fortifying."

"Perfect timing," Tessa said, reaching into the cupboard for wine glasses for herself and her neighbour.

"Bloody hell, it smells good in here." Sonya perched herself on a bar stool and peered over at the dishes in the sink. "What did you make? And are there any leftovers?"

Tessa pulled the elastic band out of her ponytail and shook her hair out, then peeled open the lid off a Tupperware container and pushed it towards her neighbour before grabbing a bag of pita crackers and a bowl.

"You're in luck. Eggplant kasundi and it's still warm."

"You, Tessa Kingsley, are a goddess." Sonya filled the glasses almost to the brim, like she always did, much to Tessa's amusement, and then sipped at the top of hers without lifting it off the bench "So why was Jerky here? I thought Abigail went to his house last weekend?"

"She did. But it's his mum's eightieth and she's having a high tea party so I made a cake for Abigail to give her. I have to pick her up tomorrow morning at seven for water polo."

"God, you're so good with your mother-in-law. I can barely stand mine. I certainly wouldn't be making her a cake if Alofa and I split up. Unless it was laced with arsenic." She scooped up some dip with her chip and put the whole thing in her mouth. "Where's Thomas? Is he working?" she asked as she chewed.

"Yep, he's doing the dinner service and then he's going out, I think, with some mates after."

"Ooh, a night to yourself. You should go out and get laid."

Tessa laughed. The idea of her going out was ridiculous, let alone the idea of finding some guy to have a one-night stand with. Between working part time in the gift shop at the garden centre, making her sauces, and running around after her kids, she couldn't remember the last time she'd even gone to the movies, let alone on a date. And since she and Keith had split almost six years ago, she'd only seen three men, both for less than a month before things fizzled out.

She picked up a pita chip and absently bit into it, before remembering her diet.

"Shit, I can't eat these," she said, going to the sink to throw the remainder out. Sonya sighed.

"Girl, you need to let go of the idea that your body isn't perfect the way it already is." She took another gulp of her wine. "All this diet crap? It's crazy. Just be you. You're gorgeous."

"That's easy for you to say, Alofa loves your body."

"He does. But most men? They love women's bodies however they come. They're not nearly as fussy or selective as you think."

"Well, Keith didn't like ..."

"Keith Jerky is a total wanker," Sonya said, cutting her off. "Do not believe anything he told you. You and I are hot curvy girls — and don't you forget it." She raised her glass. Tessa raised hers too, spilling some onto the bench.

"Here's to curvy girls," she said, but her heart wasn't really in it.

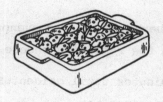

Family Potato Bake

··

Ingredients:

6 large potatoes, peeled and sliced

1 cup thickened cream

1 cup sour cream

2 tsp crushed garlic

1 1/2 cups grated cheese

handful of chopped herbs (chives, parsley, spring onion)

herbs to garnish

Method:

Preheat the oven to 180℃.

In a large pot, parboil the potatoes for 10—15 minutes until they are just soft.

Combine cream, sour cream, garlic and 1 cup of cheese in a bowl and then gently mix in the potatoes and herbs. Pour into ovenproof dish and sprinkle with the remaining cheese.

Bake for 25 minutes until golden. Sprinkle with more herbs and serve hot.

Tessa

Tessa had worked at Forests Garden Centre for five years, starting after she'd split up with Keith and was no longer doing the books for his landscaping business. He'd packed a sad about that, not understanding why she couldn't keep on doing the accounts after they'd separated. It told Tessa a lot about what their relationship meant to him: someone who would cook and clean and act as an accounts person. She had no idea what he did with the books now and didn't care.

She loved walking through the nursery, the plants lush and verdant with that fresh, earthy smell, to get to the small gift shop tucked away in a sunny corner near the tills. Tessa's boss, Prisha, was her co-worker and had become a good friend over the years. It was Prisha who had encouraged Tessa to cut down to part-time hours when she had come into work tired and stressed from staying up all night cooking, filling orders and rushing to courier them off. In fact, Prisha was the one who had encouraged her to start Taste of Tessa in the first place, after receiving Christmas and birthday gifts of homemade goodies each year. She'd set up a meeting with their purchasing team and now Tessa's products were stocked in all six branches of the garden centre. That was why if Prisha made a suggestion, Tessa listened to her.

"I wish we had more space to stock your full range." Prisha was shelving one of Tessa's best sellers, her 'Decadent Chocolate Sauce'. "I'm always having people come in and ask where they can buy your other products. You need to set up a better website. You haven't upgraded since you started and, I hate to say it, it's pretty shit."

Tessa groaned. "I know, I'm so bad at techy things though."

"That's why you pay people to do the jobs you can't. How are orders going anyway?"

"They're fine. I need to make some more time for marketing and I've had some interest from CoHab Wholefoods to stock a trial range, but you're right about the website. It's a bit of an embarrassment."

"Tessa, that's great. If you could get into a place like CoHab, they're going places. You know, maybe it's time to shoot your shot. You should think about concentrating on the business full time."

It had crossed her mind, but as much as the idea excited Tessa it also terrified her. She needed to see an increase in sales before she could confidently make that step.

A customer came up wanting Tessa to gift wrap a hand lotion for her aunt's ninetieth birthday, so she put the idea out of her mind for the time being and spent the next ten minutes talking about the price of tomatoes — "I used to grow my own" — and bunions — "You have no idea how long it takes to get an appointment to see a podiatrist. It's absolutely ridiculous."

They had a bit of a lull after that and Prisha took a coffee break, followed by Tessa. Sitting in the staffroom with Len, one of the garden centre workers, she made small talk about his cat and choked down her cottage cheese and celery sticks and forced herself to drink a litre of water before she headed back to work. On her way back she stopped in at the storeroom and picked up a carton of coloured resin paperweights inlaid with flowers which, for some reason, had been flying out the door, then headed back to the shop.

The front of the gift shop had been made to look like a garden shed, but with full panelled windows to let the light in and give customers a glimpse of what was inside. The door was cobalt blue, the paint then immediately distressed to look like it was in need of a repaint and propped permanently open. The bell alerted them to the arrival of a customer soon after Tessa had arrived back.

"Gosh, Tessa. I forget you work in this little shop. How are you?"

Tessa looked up from where she'd been arranging the paperweights as artistically as she could and plastered a fake smile on her face. "Racquel. Nice to see you. Hello, Kael."

The little boy gazed up at Tessa with pale-blue eyes, very

much like those of his father, and a sullen look. He was a tiny kid for his age, skinny like his mother with pasty skin.

"We've had a lovely little walk, haven't we, Kael, and now we're going to spend the afternoon planting some yummy lettuces and broccoli. It's so important for children to learn where their food comes from and what is in it exactly. You can't trust anything that comes in a package."

Prisha cleared her throat. "You would have passed the seedlings on your way in, Racquel. Not sure how you could have missed them."

"Yes, yes, I know. I thought I'd pop in and say hello." Racquel flicked her long blonde ponytail over one slim shoulder. Tessa noticed that her exercise gear and sports shoes matched perfectly. They always did. It was a mild source of irritation to her that her ex-husband's 'new' wife had briskly walked an hour to get here and didn't even appear to have broken out in a sweat. She *was* a gym and Pilates instructor though. She was no doubt also very flexible.

"You must come in and have a look at what Abby and I have done to her room next time you drop her off. She loves her own adult space. It's probably why she enjoys being at our place so much. Perhaps you could come for dinner one night and see?"

Tessa thought it could also be the constant requests for Abigail to babysit that meant she spent so much time there, and, honestly, she could think of nothing she'd like less than joining them all for dinner. Maybe a double root canal. It wasn't that Racquel was a totally awful person. More that they had absolutely nothing in common, other than being or having been married to the same man.

"I'm not sure when. We're so busy," Racquel rambled on. Her eyes lit on Tessa's products, prominently displayed in the middle of the shop. "Your little sauces. How lovely of Forests to sell them here for you." She picked up a jar of Orange and Kumquat marmalade, read the label and wrinkled her nose. "Have you thought of doing a low-fat, sugar-free range of products? It's the way to go these days. Nobody is eating sugar any more, Tessa. It's dreadfully out of mode." Delicately, Racquel placed the jar back on the shelf, as though touching it could make her gain five kilos, and reached for the fancy jogging buggy. "We could all do with a bit less fat and sugar, couldn't we? Kael has nothing processed in his diet."

Tessa noticed Kael now had his index finger jammed up his nose. She hoped he'd wipe the contents on his shirt when he'd finished examining them.

"Anyhoo, must dash, lovely to see you." Racquel spun the buggy around and was gone with barely a squeak of her pink and black Nikes before Tessa had a chance to answer.

• • •

When Tessa arrived home that afternoon and was sitting with a cup of tea, carefully avoiding the packet of chocolate biscuits in the pantry, she thought about what Prisha had said. Dragging out her laptop she opened up her website. It was very basic, there was no denying it. Tessa had set it up herself when she'd started out and hadn't had money spare to pay someone to do anything to it. The photos were all taken on her phone camera and weren't the best quality. They didn't show the products in their best light. Perhaps it *would* be worth the investment to get something professionally done. She googled a few web designers but had no idea what she was looking for. Someone local would be nice, not too edgy but something modern and appealing. She rejected a few choices before settling on one because he had a friendly-looking face and a nice smile and the hourly price wouldn't cripple her, and flicked off a quick email.

• • •

Thomas came in as Tessa was contemplating the contents of the pantry, carrying his knife kit under one arm. "Hey, Mum, how's things? Man, I overslept, I've gotta run."

"Do you want dinner before you go? I can make something quick. Maybe an omelette?"

"Mum," he sighed, already headed for the back door. "I work in a restaurant. You don't need to feed me."

"Force of habit," she said. She wanted to tousle the mess of his shaggy, fair hair like she had when he was small but he towered over her now and was built like a bear. He paused at the door to wedge his feet into his work Crocs.

"Well, you might not have to worry about any of my habits for much longer. I was talking to Aidan at work and his flatmate is moving out. He said I could move in with him if I wanted to."

Tessa felt her heart lurch. "You don't have to do that. I'm quite happy to have you at home." She meant it too. Thomas had the kind of easy-going, sunny personality that made him a delight to be around.

"Yeah, I know, but I'm twenty."

"Rent is so expensive though. You can save more money living here."

Thomas shrugged, picking up his car keys. "I don't need to save money though, do I? I'm not in any rush to buy a house or anything and I'm not much of a traveller."

"Still ..." She didn't know what else to say, and felt a bit lost at the thought of his moving away. It was bound to happen eventually, she knew that, but she'd miss him.

"Anyway," he said, jangling his keys, "I'll see you later. I'll probably head out after work so I'll catch you tomorrow, yeah?"

Tessa watched him go, feeling a bit mournful, and then turned her attention to dinner. Abigail also had water polo practice after school and typically arrived home starving, so Tessa made a potato bake and popped it in the oven, tossed together a salad and marinated some steaks in a new concoction she was trying out, adding in an extra piece of sirloin for her mother, Vanda.

It was a long-standing arrangement that Vanda would pick

Abigail up from practice on Tuesdays and she usually stayed for dinner and a glass of wine. Tessa was lucky that her mum was such an involved grandmother. Keith's mum was lovely but had lived out of town when the kids were younger. Now, although she lived closer, she was in a rest home and not in the best of health. Tessa appreciated all her mother's help, especially after her divorce when she was trying to juggle work and family life on her own. No matter what Vanda was going through in her own life — and she had an active social life herself — she was always there for Tessa and the kids. And for Tessa's brother, Brady, as well. Abigail especially loved her. Sometimes Tessa felt slightly jealous that her daughter seemed to confide more in her grandmother than she did her these days. But she remembered what it was like to be a teenager, when your parents really weren't that cool and didn't know anything, because it had been decades since they were young themselves.

Vanda's bright-yellow Suzuki Swift jolted into the driveway narrowly missing the letterbox. Her mother got out of the passenger seat and Tessa sighed as Abigail slammed the driver's door and hefted her backpack and gear bag out of the back seat, before clomping up the stone cobbled path. Her mother had the patience of a saint. Abigail was not a natural driver and had failed her restricted licence for the second time recently, but Vanda persuaded her to drive as often as possible, while she sat, face impassive, gripping the passenger seat.

"Polo gear in the wash, Abs," Tessa told her as Abigail dumped her bag on the kitchen table. It was the same every week. Abigail sighed and rolled her eyes, took her swimsuit and towel out and went into the laundry.

"How was school?" Tess called through to her.

"Fine, I guess."

"And practice?"

"Fine." Abigail came back into the kitchen, pulling her hair from its scrunchie. She looked so much like Tessa, but hated when anyone mentioned that.

"Are you staying, Mum?" Tessa asked.

"I'd love to, darling, if you have enough. Shall I pour us a wine? How was your day?"

"It was good. I got some meat rubs made up and packaged. Oh, and I saw Racquel and Kael in the shop today." She addressed the last comment to Abigail. "She told me you've been decorating your room at Dad's."

Abigail's face brightened. "Yeah. Also, I was talking to Dad about uni. He said he'll help pay my fees for the halls of residence next year, and Racquel's offered to take me to the open day later next semester."

"I'm happy to take you to have a look. Actually, I'd like to."

Abigail shrugged and sniffed the air. "What's for dinner anyway?"

"I'm trying out a new marinade, so steak, and I've put a potato bake in the oven. It'll be another fifteen minutes."

Abigail groaned. "Muuum, you know I don't eat carbs now."

This was news to Tessa. Potato bake had always been one of Abigail's favourites. "Well, you can have steak and salad then."

...

Later, when the dishes had been done, Vanda had gone home and Abigail was upstairs doing her homework, Tessa sat in her newly remodelled kitchen and thought about the future. Next year Abigail would be off at university and it seemed there was a good chance Thomas would have left home as well. She couldn't mope around at home missing them, and she wanted to contribute to Abigail's expenses too. There wasn't a better time to concentrate on her burgeoning business than now.

Abigail

I have my period and I'm worried that I've leaked so I keep going into the loos to check. I'm paranoid after that time Nat got hers and it ran down her leg after she got out of the pool. I'm so glad we have red swimsuits too because at least it doesn't show up as much if you bleed a bit. St Angus have white suits. They're the worst.

I'm still in the cubicle when Maddy and the others come in to get changed. That's when I hear Maddy say; "Whoa, Tiff, are you pregnant?"

"What? No."

"It's just that your stomach totally looks pregnant today," Maddy says and someone snickers.

"Fuck off, you bitch," Tiff says and Maddy laughs.

"I'm only kidding, God, don't be so sensitive."

But my stomach is way bigger than Tiff's is. I need to lose some weight. I weigh heaps more than Maddy. I think I might go on a diet. Maddy is lucky because she is tiny.

I can hear some of the girls leaving but for some reason

I stay in the cubicle. I check to make sure I haven't got any stray pubes hanging out and I make sure my hair is all under my cap and then I wait. If I go out now, Maddy will probably say something like 'Eww, were you doing a poo in there?' because I've been in here for too long.

I can hear everyone going out into the corridor and I wait. There's someone in the cubicle next door and then I hear them sniff. I think they're crying. When I come out, the only bag left on the bench is Tiff's. I want to say something but I can't think what. I feel sorry for her. She's a good goalie too.

Dad picks me up after practice. I ask if I can drive but he says he's in a rush. He never wants me to drive his new truck. When we get back to his house, Kael runs out to see me. He's wearing cute pyjamas with penguins all over them.

"Abby, watch me do happy feet," he says and then he does this hilarious tap dancing kind of jumping around and then claps his hands three times. He's so cute.

"That was awesome," I tell him.

"Can we do the story tonight?" he asks. He asks this every week when I go over. He loves it. We've been adding on to the same story for about three months now. Sometimes when I'm doing gym training, I think up things to add to it while I cycle.

"Dinner first," Racquel tells him, "and then cosmic yoga." Kael, Racquel and Dad all do yoga in the evening. It's a bit weird seeing Dad doing it but Racquel says it's good for flexibility so I usually do it too. Racquel is super fit and skinny and she can stretch so much that I feel all fat and unbendy.

We have stir-fry for dinner. Racquel makes stir-fry a lot. With tofu or chicken, lots of vegetables and konjac noodles. It's okay but I get a bit sick of stir-fry. I don't think she can cook a lot else. Sometimes we have fish and salad, or soup. When Dad cooks he does steak, baked kumara and asparagus.

"How was practice?" Dad asks.

"All right."

"What's the story with the game this weekend?"

"It's a Sunday game at Central, but Gran said she'll take me." Dad is pretty good at taking me to games but not on Sundays. I can't wait to get my licence so I can drive myself.

"We were hoping you might be able to babysit Saturday afternoon," Racquel says. "We have a class at two."

I don't mind babysitting so much but Racquel asks me just about every time I'm here. It's a bit of a pain. Kael is cute and I love him, but it's annoying having to watch him all the time.

"Maddy and I were going to go shopping," I tell her.

"Well, Kael can go with you, we can drop you off." She says it so I can't argue.

Sometimes I wonder if people think Kael is mine when I take him out with me. Like I'm a teen mum.

He's pretty good, but Racquel doesn't let him have sugar or processed food and if he wants ice cream or something and I have to say no, it seems mean. Not that I should be having ice cream either, I guess, if I want to lose weight.

"I was thinking I might go on a diet," I say.

Racquel nods. "Well, I can help you with that, I think that it's a good idea. Your dad has to watch what he eats because of his build too and you don't want to end up overweight like your mum." She starts going on about carbs and fasting and stuff and says she will write some things down, which is cool. She's a gym instructor so she knows her stuff, I guess.

She and Dad met at one of her spin classes. After he and Mum split up, they started dating and now Dad goes to the gym quite a lot. He's pretty fit and it's mainly because of Racquel.

· · ·

After baby yoga, Kael gets Jack Rabbit and comes to get me. I'm supposed to be doing homework but Maddy texted me to say that apparently Carina gave Dex a blowjob at the party last Friday and Gaia found out. She says Gaia is going to waste Carina at school tomorrow. Major drama.

I text her 'brb' and go into Kael's room. He has a teepee bed that's cute but sits low to the ground so I sort of climb in with him and we start the story. He likes to play with my hair while I talk and he rubs the end of it across his nose while he sucks on the end of Jack's ear. He's four now, but he only just got rid of his pacifier and poor Jack seems to have replaced it.

"Where were we?" I ask him.

"The mouse has landed on the moon," he says.

"Right. So Morty Mouse gets out of his rocket and he steps

out on the moon. He's very happy to discover it is made of cheese."

"Mice eat cheese," Kael says. "And peanut butter."

"They do. But then, guess what happens?"

"What?"

"It's that holey cheese and Morty falls down a big hole."

"Why?"

"Because he wasn't looking where he was going."

"Why?"

"Because he has a big space helmet on."

"Why?"

"Because you need them in space."

Kael asks 'Why?' a lot. Racquel is insistent that it's important to answer all his questions properly and give him lots of information but sometimes I can't be bothered.

"Anyway, he's stuck in a hole. So do you know what he does?"

"What?"

"He starts to eat the cheese to make a tunnel. But his tummy is getting bigger and bigger the more cheese he eats."

Kael giggles. He has such a cute laugh.

"We don't eat cheese," he says. "Only goat ones."

...

I don't usually sleep over at Dad's during the week but I am tonight because Dad is dropping off my science project for me in the morning and I've been doing it at his place. It's a hydroponic versus soil watering system and it's too bulky to move around. It's due tomorrow but I still haven't done my conclusion.

When Kael is asleep I go back to my room to get it done. My room at Dad's is cool. Racquel and I did it up and it has an outdoorsy vibe with a mint green feature wall and a nice desk area. My room at home is crap. It's so pink and babyish. This one is heaps cooler. I even have a make-up mirror in the bathroom, though I have to share the bathroom with Kael so I also have a Power Rangers step stool by the loo.

...

I check my phone before bed and Maddy has texted me to say she might ask out Dex now. He'll probably say yes. Maddy is the hottest girl in school and she can get any guy she wants. I tell her that and she texts back, 'I am sooo not. And u r hot too' with a fire emoji. Then she adds, 'I cld suss if Logan likes u?' Logan is Dex's friend. He's a bit of a weirdo.

'Maybe,' I text back.

...

I can't sleep, so I do my manifesting thing where I imagine myself on the New Zealand water polo team. We're being given medals and I'm on the podium in the team swimsuit with a tracksuit over the top. I'm skinnier and my hair is out and looks good and I smile while they take photos of us. One day, I think. One day.

Lamb Marrakech

....

Ingredients:

lamb, cut into 4 cm cubes

oil for cooking

2 diced onions

3 cloves garlic

1/2 cup raisins soaked in 1/2 cup brandy (or hot water)

1 cup chicken stock

2 Tbsp tomato paste

1 can chopped tomatoes

1 Tbsp honey

cornstarch to thicken if required

Marinade:

2 tsp paprika

1/4 tsp turmeric

1/2 tsp cumin

26

1/4 tsp cayenne pepper

1 tsp cinnamon

1/4 tsp ground cloves

1/2 tsp cardamom

1 tsp salt

1/2 tsp ground ginger

1 pinch saffron

1/4 tsp garlic powder

1/4 tsp coriander

zest of a lemon

Method:

Marinate the lamb cubes in the spices and lemon zest with a small amount of oil. Leave at least 2 hours, or even overnight.

Preheat the oven to 160℃.

Sear the lamb in oil and then add the onion and garlic and sauté 5 minutes before adding the rest of your ingredients.

Place in a tagine or casserole dish and slow cook in the oven for around 2 hours.

Serve with couscous, prunes or dried apricots, chopped coriander and roasted slithered almonds.

Tessa

Seth Barker was prematurely grey and wiry with nails bitten to the quick. He seemed skittish and reminded Tessa of a rescue greyhound Abigail had begged her to adopt a few years ago. They met at the cafe within the garden centre on her lunch break and she was a little amused when he ordered a lime milkshake, telling her coffee made him antsy. She suspected most things made him antsy and wondered if he had ADHD like Thomas's friend Jake. He fidgeted with the sugar sachets while they waited for the drinks, his knee bouncing continuously. It wasn't until he opened his laptop and looked at her website that he stilled, his focus intense.

He had some good ideas. He showed her some ways to make ordering easier and how to connect her invoicing to make it a less labour-intensive process. He suggested better fonts and adding links to social media, which he insisted she needed to improve.

"Instagram is your best bet," he told her, sipping his

drink and leaving a milk moustache on his upper lip. "But you need way better pictures. For Insta and your site. Visual marketing is ninety-five per cent more effective than text. These are terrible. Sorry, but they are."

It was true. Tessa had taken some okay shots of her products but the lighting was a bit off, and they didn't pop, despite her lovely labels.

"I have a friend who's a photographer, if you want his number? He's a good guy. I went to school with him. I designed his web page too." He tapped on the keyboard and brought up a site. It was a very artful page and the photos were stunning, even to Tessa's untrained eye. "He does it part time, and his rates are pretty good. He did my sister's wedding. His name's Chris. Chris Bacon. Let me give him a call."

...

She was putting the tagine of lamb into the oven to slow cook when someone on a fancy racing bike pulled up outside her gate and dismounted. He had very nice cyclist's legs, she noted, as he took off his helmet and gave his hair a quick ruffle before taking something from the saddle bag. As he meandered up the path, she looked at the time on her phone, realised it must be the photographer, and removed her apron before giving herself a quick glance in the hall mirror. Lucky, because her right cheek had a streak of flour on it and her hair was a disaster. She did a rushed tidy up before going to the door.

He was bent over at the base of the steps, inspecting a gnome that lay flat on the grass, a knife protruding from its back. When he looked up, he grinned.

"Great gnome."

He was rather gorgeous, Tessa noted. Younger than her and lean, with light-brown hair that was receding at the top and the patchy start of a beard. He had hazel eyes and olive skin and he held out a nicely muscled arm to shake her hand.

"Chris Bacon," he said. "Are you Tessa?"

"That's me." She was feeling a bit flustered and wishing she'd made a bit more effort with her appearance. There was an oil stain on her T-shirt, and she crossed her arms to cover it. "Please come in."

"Something smells amazing."

"It's Lamb Marrakesh. My brother is coming over for dinner and it's his favourite."

"Right, could be that," he said, leaning in rather close to her as they stood in the kitchen. "But I think it's you. Is that Jo Malone you're wearing?"

"What? No." Tessa raised her wrist to her nose and sniffed. "I don't think I have perfume on today."

Chris leant in and smelt her wrist too. He was close to her, his breath on her skin sending a weird little jolt of friction up her arm.

"Whatever it is, it's great. Like poached pears."

"Body lotion," Tessa said, her voice a bit breathless. "Ecoya, I think."

There was a bit of an awkward pause while they both

stood in her kitchen, him smiling at her and her feeling like she was bright red and about fourteen.

"Right, well, can I offer you a drink?" she finally managed to ask.

"Water would be great. I forgot to fill up my bottle before I set off."

"Please, have a seat." She indicated the long bench with bar stools and went to fill two glasses, bringing them back and taking a seat herself. He had the camera out and was taking a shot of the pretzels she had made the day before that sat under a domed stand on her counter.

"You have fantastic lighting in here for food shots." He held out the camera for her to see the image.

"Wow, they look so much better than they are."

"They look pretty good anyway, but it's all in the angle and focus." He took a gulp of his water. "I blurred the background a bit. It gives them a bit of a pop. Did you make them?"

"Yes. Only for snacks, not for work." Something in his tone made her add, "Help yourself if you'd like one."

He took one without hesitation, biting into it and groaning appreciatively. "Bloody hell, these are great. Your partner's a lucky specimen."

"Yeah, no. No specimen here." Tessa looked down and fiddled with her glass.

"Right, well, where do I apply?" Tessa looked up and Chris gave her a cheeky wink. "But honestly, if all your food looks this good, photos will be easy. What products are you wanting highlighted? Tell me what you're looking for."

It was a relief to get down to business. Tessa was sure he was just being friendly, but it had felt a bit flirty and she was out of her element in that regard. She ran Chris through her product range of sauces, chutneys and dressings and then showed him some of the products she had on hand.

"Nice labels," he told her, holding up the chocolate sauce. "But have you thought about photographing these a bit differently?"

"How do you mean?"

"Well, I'm thinking, as a point of interest, instead of the usual shots of the bottle, we could do some where they've been used as you intend them to be. The chocolate sauce, for example, we could do it over ice cream, or not — that's a bit overdone." He rubbed his palm across his stubble. "What about as a dip with churros? Can you make churros?"

"Yes, I could." Tessa thought a bit about it herself. It was a good idea. All her pictures were only of the bottles and jars, and he had a good point. They didn't stand out from the crowd. "What about cream puffs? In a big stack?"

"Perfect. I think we could come up with some great images for the other products too. If you were happy we could start with cream puffs and go from there. I could come back one evening this week if that suited. Or the weekend?

They discussed pricing and Tessa was pleasantly surprised by his fees. They arranged for him to come back the next Friday afternoon and Tessa would have the cream puffs ready for their debut photo shoot.

"Wear something bright, and not too patterned or busy," Chris told her. "Avoid black if you can. And no logos unless it's yours."

"Wait. What? What for? Surely I don't need to be in the shot?" Tessa said, her voice raising in panic. "I look awful in photos."

"No, you won't," Chris said very calmly. "You'll look amazing. Trust me. And you do want a picture of you on the page. It helps people feel connected to you and the brand."

Tessa tried not to freak out. She hated photos of herself. She looked so dumpy. She was the one who offered to take the photo, or the one who stood in the back of the group, despite being so short.

"I promise, you'll look great," Chris said. "You've got a fantastic face. Amazing eyes."

Tessa thought that was nice, but she heard that a lot. What else could people say? They were hardly going to compliment her body.

"Well, I'd better get going, I suppose." Chris stood and stretched, his T-shirt riding up and exposing his lower stomach and that lovely line of happy trail. Tessa stared a little too long, then quickly looked away.

"Thank you so much for coming so quickly," she said. He did a funny little cough and she looked up to see him grinning.

"Not a problem, Tessa," he said. "It was my pleasure."

Thomas's No-bake
Chocolate Tart
·······································

Ingredients:

200 g pack of plain biscuits

100 g butter

1 Tbsp golden syrup or honey

100 g bar dark chocolate

100 g bar milk chocolate

1 tsp vanilla extract

2 Tbsp icing sugar, plus extra for dusting

200 ml whipping cream

3 Tbsp crème fraîche to decorate

200 g raspberries to serve

Method:

Crush the biscuits by putting them in a large, strong, plastic food bag and bashing with a rolling pin. Melt the butter with the syrup or honey in the microwave, then stir it into the biscuits. Press the mix onto the base and up the sides of a 12 x 36 cm rectangular tin (or 23—25 cm round flan tin) and chill it while you make the filling.

Break up the two chocolate bars and put them in a large bowl. Melt in the microwave for 2—3 minutes on medium power, stirring halfway through. Stir in the vanilla extract, then sift in the icing sugar. Whip the cream until it just holds its shape, then fold it into the melted chocolate. Pour the mix into the prepared tin and smooth the top. Chill for at least 2 hours or for up to 2 days.

Just before serving, remove the tart from the tin and slide it onto a flat plate. (Loosen the edges first with the tip of a knife. You may find it easier to remove the tart if you leave it at room temperature for 30 minutes.) Put a few tablespoons of crème fraîche along the centre of the tart (or around the edges if the tart is circular) and top each with a raspberry, then dust lightly with icing sugar. Cut into thin slices and serve.

Tessa

Brady pulled up in his truck as Chris pedalled off around the corner. He got out and slung a large duffel bag over his broad shoulder, before going over and leaning heavily against Keith's landscaping sign for a bit. It swayed slightly, one leg raising a little and setting it on a lean, and he grinned widely. Thomas looked a lot like Brady, big and soft, thought Tessa, as he ambled up to her door with his big boots and his baggy jeans, whistling tunelessly.

"Hey, sis." He picked her up and hugged her tight, enveloping her in his woody scent. "Hope you don't mind but I brought my laundry again. The part for my machine still hasn't arrived."

"Only if you plan to do it. I have enough washing of my own, I'm not doing yours too."

"Where are the kids? I have some tickets to the women's rugby I thought they might want."

"I'm sure they will. They should be back soon. Thomas

36

finishes at six today and Keith is picking Abs up after practice. God, you have a great job."

"Yeah, the perks are awesome."

Brady was a freelance sports journalist and also a part-time commentator. He was a very favourite uncle to her kids, who were both sports fans, especially Abigail. Thomas, she suspected, enjoyed the games more because he loved spending time with Brady. Tessa was not a sports fan. As kids, Brady was popular. Good at almost every sport, playing rugby, softball and basketball and a part of the school rowing team, while Tessa couldn't catch a ball without flinching.

"I'll throw this in the machine then," Brady said, heading off to the laundry. "But I'd murder my father for a beer. Mackenzie has me doing Dry February and it's killing me having to sneak drinks in without her knowing."

Mackenzie was the latest in a long line of girlfriends. She was a sports therapist Brady had met at work and Tessa wasn't overly keen on her. She was pleased that Brady never brought her round to their weekly dinners. They'd been going out almost three months, so she suspected she would be on her way out soon in any case. Probably before February was over. She rummaged in the fridge and found a couple of craft beers and grabbed some tumblers, putting them on the table and sitting down. Opening a beer for herself, she poured it down the side of the glass, the smell of hops and citrus rising up.

"Any idea what this thing is Mum wants us to go to next

Saturday?" Brady asked as he came back and nabbed the glass from her. "It's a bit of a fancy venue." She whacked his arm and poured out the other one for herself. He helped himself to a pretzel.

"Nope. She just said to make sure we all came and to dress 'nicely'. Could be anything, knowing Vanda."

"Weird. Maybe something to do with the jewellers?" Vanda had worked part time at a high-end store called Jennings Jewellers for years. She didn't need to — her second marriage and widowing had left her financially well off — but she liked to keep busy and said she enjoyed the interaction with the customers.

"Can't imagine what," Tessa said, sipping her beer. "She's being a bit cagey about it."

"Still, it's Vanda, she's often weird. She keeps dropping off ladders to my house."

"Oh God, me too. What the hell is with that? Is she running a building supplies racket? First, I got a stepladder, which is actually handy, but then she turned up with a great big outdoor one that folds down or something."

"A telescoping ladder. She's given me one too. I had to tell her no man needs three ladders in an apartment building. I'm six foot four, for crying out loud. Good pretzels, by the way."

The front door opened and Thomas, Abigail and Keith piled in, all talking over the top of each other. Brady got up and gave the kids a hug. Tessa watched enviously, wishing

Abigail would still hug her like that. She'd been so free with hugs when she was a little girl but now Tessa couldn't remember the last time Abigail had hugged her of her own free will. Usually it was with arms plastered to her sides, or with barely touching hands on Tessa's back, like it was a duty to be endured.

"Dinner in ten," she told them, getting up to sort the couscous and take the hot tagine out of the oven. They traipsed off to their rooms, carrying sports gear and knife kits. Thomas placed a cake box on the bench as he passed. Keith and Brady shook hands.

"All right, mate?" Brady asked Keith. "How's life?"

"Can't complain," Keith said. "No one listens anyway." He laughed at his own joke, but his tone seemed off to Tessa. Still, not her problem, was it, unless it was about the kids. He eyed the tagine on the bench like a man who hadn't eaten for a week. "All right with you if I come and do some work on the grounds on Sunday?" he asked her. "It could do with a bit of a tidy. Some pruning. That sort of thing."

"Knock yourself out," she told him. "So long as the gnomes stay where they are."

He gave her a very salty look and left, pulling the front door shut firmly behind him.

Brady laughed. "Are you still trying to piss him off with those gnomes?"

"Well, it's working, isn't it? But don't tell the kids. I don't want them to think there's too much animosity between us.

Nothing worse than parents who obviously don't get on after a split."

"Wouldn't know about that," Brady said and they both cracked up. It was laugh or cry. Their own father had left them all when Brady was a toddler and Tessa was about to turn four. She only vaguely remembered it all, her mother crying all over the fairy bread at her party and a hazy sense that he had been an angry drunk of a man. He died in a car accident a few years later. One of the reasons Tessa thought she'd hung on to her dying marriage so long was wanting to have the stability of a unified family for her own children. She'd been devastated when Keith had left, more for Thomas and Abigail than for herself.

"Yes, well, I think it's time to stop blaming your lack of commitment on your abandonment issues and admit that you need to stop dating vapid young girls." Tessa threw the toasted almonds on top of her finished dish and carried it to the table.

"And I think you need to get laid," Brady retorted, going over to the cupboard to grab the plates.

"Gross," Abigail said, plonking herself down at the table and rolling her eyes. "Can we not talk about old people having sex?" Brady pretended to have been shot, crumpling dramatically.

"Hey, enough of the old, thank you very much. We're not dead yet."

"Not you," Abigail said. "But no one wants to think about

their parents doing it, trust me."

"True that," he agreed.

"I made chocolate tarts today and there's some for later," Thomas said as he pulled out a chair. Tessa placed the steamed green beans on the table and sat down too.

"Oh my God, why does everyone keep cooking so much unhealthy stuff all the time?" Abigail complained dramatically. "There's so many carbs in this house. No wonder everyone is fat."

"Wow, settle down," Thomas said mildly.

"Shut up, Tom," she fired back.

"Okay, okay," Brady interjected, holding up both hands like twin stop signs. "I have tickets to the rugby, who's in?"

Tessa reminded herself not to have a tart after dinner, and put a smaller than usual scoop of couscous on her plate.

Baklava

~~~~~~~~

Ingredients:

500 g filo pastry

1 cup melted butter, plus more for greasing the pan

450 g nuts (almonds, walnuts or pistachios are best, or use a combination of them), finely chopped

1/3 cup sugar

1 tsp ground cinnamon

1/3 tsp ground cloves

finely ground pistachios to garnish (optional)

Syrup:

1 cup water

1 cup sugar

1/2 cup honey

2 Tbsp lemon juice

1 cinnamon stick

Method:

Preheat the oven to 180°C.

Keep the pastry sheets under a damp tea towel to avoid them drying out.

Lightly grease a 23 x 33 cm pan.

In a food processor, pulse the nuts until they are finely chopped. Combine with the sugar, cinnamon and cloves.

In a separate bowl, melt the butter in the microwave.

Place a sheet of filo into the pan. Using a pastry brush, brush the filo sheet with melted butter. Repeat 7 more times until it is 8 sheets thick, each sheet being 'painted' with the butter.

Spoon on a thin layer of the nut mixture. Cover with 2 more sheets of filo, brushing each one with butter. Continue to repeat the nut mixture and 2 buttered sheets of filo until the nut mixture is all used up. The top layer should be 8 filo sheets thick, each sheet being individually buttered. (Don't worry if the sheets crinkle up a bit; it will add more texture.)

Cut into 24 equal-sized squares using a sharp knife.

Bake for 30–35 minutes or until lightly golden brown, and edges appear slightly crisp.

While baking, make the syrup.

Combine all ingredients in a saucepan. Bring to a boil, then reduce to medium-low heat and let simmer for 7 minutes until slightly thickened. Remove the cinnamon stick and allow it to cool.

Spoon the cooled syrup over the hot baklava and let it cool, uncovered, for at least 4 hours.

Garnish with some finely ground pistachios, if using.

Eleni

Eleni sat in her car, parked in the driveway outside her house, and sighed. Her feet ached and she had a burn on her wrist, from the iron, that had started to blister. Behind the beige linen curtains of her lounge, she could see the TV flickering and the shadow of Theo pacing back and forward behind the couch. She felt so weary.

Savvas was home, his station wagon parked in the garage, but he wouldn't have started dinner or given Theo his meds, or even put his lunch dishes in the dishwasher. She could envision him easily, sitting in his chair, feet up, a can of beer on the arm rest, telling Theo to stop with the racket. He insisted the stimming was a bad habit that needed correcting, no matter how many times she told him it was part of his disorder.

Her boss, Howard, had asked her to stay late tonight, to talk about what he called 'a sensitive issue'. She had been distracted all afternoon, worrying that it would be about

44

her last job. About the termination. But instead he'd sat her down and asked her if she could do him a favour.

She blushed to her roots, thinking about his request. Tried to imagine herself going into the pharmacy and asking for them. Viagra.

Would they think it was for her? Did women even take it? She didn't think so, but wasn't sure. Would they think it was for Savvas? He would be horrified if he thought people believed he couldn't get it up. She laughed softly to herself at the idea. She would get Howard his pills, even though she would be mortified to do it. She was Howard's caregiver, after all. His nurse. That word made her feel like an imposter.

Still, Howard was over eighty. She hadn't even known he had a girlfriend. Or perhaps he didn't? Perhaps he was paying for sex? But she had worked for him for years now, known him all her life, and he'd never seemed that sort. He was a nice man.

Her mother, Cora, had been Howard's housekeeper when Eleni was a child. Eleni had grown up with Donald and his sister, Annette, though they'd barely acknowledged her, being much younger and the mere daughter of the housekeeper, going to the house after school where she would watch her mother in their flash kitchen, surrounded by other children she treated like her own. Though Howard and his wife, Ruth, had always been kind to her.

After Ruth had died, Donald and his wife, Margot, had moved in for a bit. Chris, Felicia and Ben were kiddies. Now

Howard's grandson Ben was living with him, although less to help Howard than himself, Eleni thought.

She still needed to bake the baklava for Mamá for tomorrow. She would take it into the rest home where her mother now lived and sit with her for a few hours while Theo was at his daycare. His 'work', as he called it. She needed to remember to pack his togs and towel for his visit to the community pool too, although he never went right in the water, just paddled in the kiddies area up to his knees. Eleni wished for once she could use her day off to do something else. Something for her.

Instead, she got out of the car and made her way up the path to her house. Resigned to her lot.

...

After she'd fed Theo dinner and given him a shower, Eleni cleaned up the mess and started on the baklava. Savvas had gone to bed. The sound of his snoring reverberated down the hallway like a lawnmower on steroids. She poured herself an ouzo and sipped it while she cut up pistachios. It was her great-grandmother's recipe and one she knew by heart. The process was soothing, layering the pastry and spooning over the filling, mindless and calming. But she was tired. While it was in the oven, Eleni made the syrup and packed Theo and Savvas's lunchboxes.

Once the kitchen was again tidied, she ran a bath and tried to let the hot water ease the knots out of her shoulders. Theo was finally asleep and she hoped tonight was a good one. One where he didn't decide at two in the morning that it was movie time. Or worse, wet the bed. Twenty-three years of wet nappies, wet undies and wet sheets. Twenty-three years.

She wondered if she should call Tobias. Check in on him. But he was so busy with his work and his friends and he sounded a little bit exasperated with her when she rang. A chore for him, to talk to his mother, much like everyone else was for her.

At night, when she tried to relax, all she could think of was Mrs Beston and her face as they resuscitated her. Doughy and pallid. She'd lived, but only just. No thanks to her. No, Eleni was to blame. Too tired and absent minded and she had nearly killed her. She hadn't double-checked the medication. How could she possibly call herself a nurse after that? She could never forgive herself for making such a silly mistake.

Eleni wondered how much longer she could go on. If it was worth trying to talk to Savvas again about a residential care unit for Theo. She knew what he would say though. That it was a mother's job to look after her children. That God never gave you more than you could cope with. He was the head of the household, and he made the decisions.

Eleni had loved her husband once. She could almost remember what it had felt like. Had Savvas changed or had life worn her down so much she was numb to any of the emotions she used to feel? She suspected he hadn't changed at all and that she'd been young and blind. Things were different back then. It wasn't so long ago but, especially the way she grew up, women accepted their lot and got on with life the best they could. Her mother had been the same, coming home after cooking and cleaning for another family, cooking and cleaning for her own. Eleni's páppa had worked ten-hour days though, not spent his time working a part-time job and then sitting around the house complaining and drinking. He'd been a good man and a hard worker.

She sank down under the water and closed her eyes, because it was the only way to stop herself from sobbing.

Pani Popo

....

Ingredients:

2 1/4 tsp active dry yeast

1–1 1/4 cups lukewarm water

3 cups flour

1/4 cup sugar

1 tsp salt

3 Tbsp unsalted butter, softened, plus more for greasing the pan

Coconut sauce:

1 cup coconut milk

1 cup water

1/2 cup sugar

Method:

In a small bowl, sprinkle yeast over 1 cup of the water and stir together. Allow to sit until frothy, about 10 minutes.

In the bowl of a stand mixer fitted with a dough hook, or a large bowl, combine the flour, sugar and salt.

Mix in the softened butter, then the frothy yeast with the water until a soft dough comes together. If it's too crumbly, add up to ¼ cup more water. If it's too sticky, add just enough flour to handle.

On a lightly floured surface, knead the dough until smooth and elastic. Place in a lightly greased large bowl, turning to coat. Cover and let rise at room temperature until doubled in size, about 2 hours.

Grease a 23 x 33 cm deep baking dish with butter.

Place dough on lightly floured surface. Roll the dough into a long rectangle, then roll up long side to long side to create a long log.

Cut the log into 12 equal spiralled rolls. Arrange the rolls in a single layer in the prepared baking dish. Cover and let rise until doubled, about 30 minutes.

Preheat the oven to 200℃.

To make the coconut sauce, in a small bowl, whisk together the coconut milk, water and sugar until well combined.

Pour the coconut sauce evenly over the tops of the buns and bake for 25—30 minutes until golden brown and the coconut sauce is bubbling.

Remove the pan from the oven and cover it with a piece of foil. Allow the buns to cool covered in the pan for 30 minutes to 1 hour before serving.

Tessa

Keith arrived early on Sunday morning before Tessa had properly woken up. The sound of the edge trimmer right outside her bedroom window had her downstairs in her bathrobe, bread in to be toasted before eight o'clock. It felt way too early, especially for the weekend. He appeared around the corner of the house as she poured her first cup of tea of the morning and she watched him work for a moment. Tessa had to admit, he was still in good shape for his age, lean and toned, only slightly bulkier than he had been when she'd first met him in their early twenties. Abigail told her Racquel had him on a strict health routine. She liked to think that was why he was such a grumpy arse these days. Keith was conscious of his body and keeping fit and it had been a bone of contention to him that Tessa wasn't. She didn't miss the birthday and Christmas gifts of hand weights and gym memberships, despite asking for hand mixers and food magazine subscriptions. Now she bought herself those kinds of things when she could afford it. Keith had a secret sweet tooth though, and Tessa was spitefully tempted to bake a chocolate brownie and crack the window open, until she thought of the silver dress. It seemed unlikely Abigail would eat any of it either. She'd probably only end up giving it away or binning the whole thing.

The toast popped up suddenly, startling her slightly, and Tessa smeared it with a thin layer of Vegemite, no butter, and took her plate and mug of black tea over to the table. She should be having her diet shake but couldn't face it.

The vision of Chris Bacon sitting across from her eating a pretzel flashed through her mind. She thought about which platter she would use to display the cream puffs for the photo shoot. Then about Chris smelling her wrist.

Tessa rinsed her plate and watched Keith lift the lawnmower from the back of his ute. She thought about Chris and his nice cycler legs. Turning from the window, she went into the laundry and started folding the week's worth of washing instead.

* * *

Keith had moved on to pruning dead wood from the avocado tree when Tessa saw Sonya crossing the garden between their houses. Years ago, Keith had built a gate between their properties. He'd got tired of Sonya and Tessa pushing through the shrubbery and ruining the look of it, but Keith and Sonya had never got on. Keith and Alofa had watched sports together sometimes, but Sonya's husband was an easy-going guy and got on with most people. He'd give Keith a wave when he saw him in the garden now, but mostly kept his distance. Sonya had nicknamed Tessa's ex 'Keith Jerky' because of his obsession with keeping fit after he and Tessa had split. When Keith had started going to the gym and met Racquel especially. That and the fact that he was a massive jerk.

Sonya gave him a brief wave now as she skipped up the stairs onto the deck. Sliding the door open without knocking, she slipped off her bright-orange slides and held out a small wicker basket covered in a checked tea towel. Her toenails were orange with tiny daisies painted onto each of her big toes, to match the footwear.

"Coconut buns."

Tessa peeked at the still-warm buns and sighed. Her stomach gurgled in appreciation. "Sonn, you know that I'm ..."

"Trying to lose weight. Yes, I know. Put the kettle on and stop being such a bloody bore." Sonya took a seat at the kitchen table and watched as Tessa flicked on the kettle and filled the teapot with hot water from the tap to warm it.

"Why do you have to wear the silver dress anyway? If it doesn't fit right, pick something else. What about that pink chiffony thing you got for my anniversary party?"

"It was Mum's suggestion. She's invited us all to this thing she's having next Saturday and is being secretive about it, except that we have to dress up. I suggested the black silk pantsuit I bought last year in the summer sales but she was insistent that the silver dress would be perfect."

"Vanda has excellent taste. If she thinks it's perfect, then it's probably perfect. Show me."

Tessa reluctantly led Sonya up to her bedroom and put the dress on.

"It looks fine to me. That crossover neckline is flattering," Sonya said as Tessa twirled awkwardly in front of her.

"My boobs look like they're about to leap out and slap someone in the face," Tessa wailed. "And it's tight around the hips."

"It's *fitted* around the hips. And your boobs look amazing. The perfect amount of cleavage to be interesting without being totally slutty. Not that I'm slut-shaming or anything, you go for it, girl. Whoever you slap in the face with those gorgeous susu is bloody lucky."

Tessa slipped off the dress and put it back on the hanger before they went downstairs for the tea.

They watched as Keith raked up branches and stuffed them into a large garden bag. Tessa cut one of the buns into four and took a piece. It was delicious. She popped the rest of the quarter into her mouth and picked up another.

"Is it wrong that I think Keith has nice arms? I mean, I wouldn't want to go back there, not in a million years, but he's still quite attractive, isn't he?"

"If you like your jerks beefy and toned, yeah, I guess. I prefer a bit of something to grab hold of myself." Sonya licked coconut off her fingers. "He's not a bad-looking guy, I'll give him that. Pity he's such an absolute tool. It's probably that you haven't had a shag in so long and you're horny as hell."

Chris came to the forefront of Tessa's mind again. She told Sonya about his visit. "It seemed like he was flirting with me, but I'm pretty sure he's quite a bit younger."

"So? Wouldn't that be perfect for a fling?"

"You know I don't do flings."

"Haven't," Sonya amended. "Doesn't mean you can't."

"I guess I'm a bit sceptical about relationships. Keith made me feel like shit. Anyone I've dated has ended up being a disappointment. I haven't met anyone else I can imagine spending the rest of my life with. Anyway, Mum's had two husbands and now she's in her seventies and alone. What's the point?"

"You don't have to marry him, just bang his brains—"

Sonya fell silent as Abigail and her friend Maddy came into the kitchen. They set about making coffee, whispering and giggling.

"You girls should have one of Sonya's pani popo. They're one of Abigail's favourite things."

Maddy eyed the plate disdainfully. "Really?" She shot Abigail a disbelieving look, as though Tessa was pointing out a plate of raw pig's ears.

"When I was little," Abigail said, going a bit pink. She adored Sonya and seemed torn between hurting her feelings and wanting to please Maddy. Perhaps family-style food wasn't very cool any more?

Sonya didn't seem to notice. "I remember when you and Levi used to lie under the fig tree in our garden with a plate of buns and eat until your stomachs hurt. I'll message him to bring the rest of the batch over." She got out her phone and sent a text.

"That's okay, you don't have to," Abigail said.

"I'm sure he won't mind at all."

Abigail fiddled with her ponytail. "I don't really eat carbs any more."

Sonya scoffed. "Carbs aren't bad for you, Abs. Everything in moderation, right?"

...

Levi didn't seem to mind. In no time at all Sonya's son was grinning at them through the sliding door. When she saw Levi, Tessa took in the tall, handsome young man who had replaced the cute young boy she remembered from when Sonya and Alofa had first moved in next door. He still had the same lovely smile, she noted. Levi handed over the buns, which he'd shoved into a paper shopping bag.

"Hi, Tessa. Hey, Abby."

"Hi, Levi." It was Maddy who answered. She gave him a little finger wave. "I'm in your visual art class, and we were in graphics last year."

"Yeah, hi, Maddy. I remember you."

Maddy giggled. "Well, yeah."

"Your self-portrait last year was cool. Do you do water

polo with Abby as well?"

"Yeah, you should come and watch sometime. If you can handle a pool full of girls."

"Might do that." Levi reached over and took a bun from the bag, then offered them to the girls, who both declined. "Better go. Got heaps of homework." He gave a little wave, but Tessa noticed he was looking at Abigail, and not at Maddy at all.

Sonya stood. "I'll come with you. I promised your dad I'd help him clean out the guttering."

"Here, take the extra buns." Tessa thrust the bag at her. "Levi will be sad if you leave them all here."

Sonya gave her a look. "Okay then, but wear the silver dress."

• • •

Tessa rinsed the plate and cups, her back to Abigail and Maddy as they giggled and sipped their coffee at the breakfast bar.

"He's so hot," Maddy said.

Tessa could see Keith out of the window, finishing up in the garden, and for an alarming minute she thought Maddy was talking about him.

"Who, Levi?" Abigail asked, snorting.

"Yeah, he's really fit. Like he was such a geek before year twelve but now – I'd totally do him."

It was funny, Tessa thought, how adults became invisible,

and deaf, if they were background fixtures in a room.

"I guess he's okay," Abigail said.

"He was totally, like, flirting with me. Did you get that vibe? Like, he probably got a boner when I said he should come to the pools. He's so going to be thinking about me in my togs now."

Abigail said nothing. Maddy was tall and slim, with a beautiful figure. She had wavy blonde hair and blue eyes. Tessa knew she weighed fifty-two kilos. Abby had told her several times.

Tessa picked up the pile of washing she'd been folding earlier and headed down the hallway.

"His mum's so stupid though," she heard Maddy say. "All that 'carbs aren't bad'. Yeah, right. Why is she so fucking fat then?"

She knew she should respond but Abigail would probably only bite her head off afterwards for embarrassing her in front of her friend, so she let it be and went upstairs to put the washing away.

The girls had gone for a 'training walk' when Tessa came back downstairs, which seemed to involve walking around the block several times, crossing in front of Levi's house and doing stretches outside in the garden facing his bedroom.

Keith knocked on the door and then stuck his head in. "All done. I'll come back in a couple of weeks and finish off. It's not like anyone else in this house will do anything to help." Tessa sighed internally. Keith hated anyone else touching his precious garden.

"It looks good," she said graciously. The property did look much nicer.

"It would look a hell of a lot better if you got rid of those stupid gnomes," he huffed. "Who's going to employ a landscaper if they think he'd put those monstrosities in their garden? Anyway, I need to take the sign out and lay some better foundations. It's on a bloody lean. Don't know why that is."

"It's a mystery," Tessa said, trying not to smile. Removing the sign was good, Tessa thought. Even if it was temporary. She was sick of people knocking on the door asking to speak to Keith about redesigning their garden. His number was right there, but often people thought this was still his place of business. Hopefully it would take a while to sort. She wished she'd never agreed to have the sign there, but the free maintenance was too good a bonus to overlook.

"Don't forget Abigail needs to be back before lunch on Saturday," she said. Abby spent a lot of time at Keith's and was babysitting next Friday night. "Have a nice anniversary dinner, by the way."

Keith ran his hand through his hair. "Yeah, thanks." He paused, and seemed to consider whatever it was he was going to say next. "Sorry for being a bit of a prick about the garden, but we've been doing IVF and it's all a bit tense at the moment. We need all the money we can get, it's not cheap."

"Sorry to hear that, Keith. Take your time with the sign," Tessa said, and he turned and stomped off down the path, muttering something about hormonal women.

Abigail

"I've lost two kilos," I tell Racquel at dinner. I'm feeling pretty proud of myself. I've been really hungry but now I'm seeing results.

"Well, that's a good start," Racquel says. I kind of thought she'd be more impressed but at least at dinner she serves me small portions. Not like Mum who gives me massive amounts of food, like, enough to feed a pigsty, which is basically what everyone in that house is.

"I'll make you one of my protein shakes for breakfast in the morning," Racquel says.

I do my homework, which helps me ignore my growling stomach, and then I do some push-ups and star jumps, which are good for training anyway. When I look at myself front on in the mirror, I think I'm looking a bit thinner, but if I stand sideways, I still look like a massive hog. I'm going to do better next week. I might start jogging.

Maddy has been so sweet and said I was doing really well

when I only had a yoghurt at school. She's so encouraging sometimes. She even said that when I can fit it, she's going to give me her green Roxy maxi dress that she knows I like.

We went to Maddy's after school yesterday and she invited Dex and Logan over. Maddy's house is cool and her mum's always at work so we drank beers from the bar fridge that her mum never checks and listened to some tunes. Luckily we didn't swim so we didn't have to get in our togs. She reckons Logan likes me but I don't know, because everyone knows he likes Maddy and he seemed pissed when she was kissing Dex and hardly talked to me. I wish they could have gone to her bedroom instead of snogging right there in front of us. It was kind of weird. What are you even meant to talk about when some guy's best friend has his tongue down your best friend's throat anyway?

* * *

Maddy's mum is chill and I like going to her place better than mine. Miranda is so stylish and my mum is like a frumpy housewife. She never has any nice clothes that I'd want to borrow or expensive jewellery. Miranda hasn't even noticed that Maddy's been wearing her gold lotus necklace for the last three months. There's no nice food at Maddy's either, so I'm not tempted. Mum's always cooking and trying to make me be as fat as her. She probably hopes nobody will ever have sex with me, and that way she can pretend I'm her little girl forever. The way I'm going, nobody will have sex with me. Not that I'd want to do it with Logan. His hair is kind of greasy and he laughs like a buffoon — 'Haw, haw, haw, haw'.

Dad and Racquel are going out *again*, but Kael is already in bed. He's been pretty good but he wants extra stories when I'm babysitting. He calls out and asks for a drink. I tell him I'll get him some water but he begs me for milk and I give in, like he knows I will. Racquel thinks cow's milk is only for baby cows so I get him oat milk, warmed up with a quarter teaspoon of manuka honey for a treat. Racquel doesn't like him having drinks at night because sometimes he wets the bed. But he tells me I'm the best sister ever and he wants to hug me and never let me go, which is pretty cute.

Once he's asleep I get out my laptop to watch something. There's a new episode of *Riverdale* but I've been thinking about how Levi came over the other day. I wonder if I should text him about hanging out. We used to hang out all the time. Does he still have the same number? Probably he'd want to hang out with Maddy too but we used to do stuff together, just the two of us. When we were little my mum invited all the neighbours over and everyone would bring food and the adults would get drunk and forget about us kids. One time Thomas fell off the deck and nobody even realised he had a broken arm until the morning. It was great.

I wish I could have eaten one of Sonya's coconut buns though. I feel bad that I didn't and I hope she wasn't upset or that Levi thought I was being a bitch. I couldn't though.

I can't focus on watching anything. Whenever I sit down

I feel like I'm gaining weight, so I do some squats and text Maddy.

'What u doing?'

While I'm waiting for her to reply I do two sets of crunchies.

'Dumped Dex. Fuckwit's gone crawling bk 2 Gaia'

I didn't even know they were going out, like officially or anything.

'Soz', I text.

'Dnt care. His fuckin loss'

I wonder how Maddy could have dumped Dex and he's already got back together with Gaia since after school today. And how she even knew they'd got back together. Here I am, I can't even bring myself to text a guy I've known for years.

"Abby," Kael calls.

I go into his room and he's wet his bed.

Cream Puffs

....

Ingredients:

75 g butter

1 cup water

150 g flour

1 Tbsp sugar

1/2 tsp vanilla essence

3 large eggs

chocolate sauce for topping

Filling:

1 cup cream

2 Tbsp icing sugar

1 tsp vanilla essence

Method:

Preheat the oven to 200℃. Place baking paper on 2 oven trays.

Bring the butter and water to the boil in a saucepan. Add the flour all at once and beat until the mixture leaves the side of the pan.

Remove from the heat and add the sugar and vanilla.

Beat in the eggs, one at a time.

Place teaspoonfuls of the mixture onto the prepared oven trays.

Bake for 15—20 minutes, until puffed and golden. Cool.

To assemble:

Beat the cream, icing sugar and vanilla with a mixer until firm.

Cut puffs in half and fill with the cream, sandwiching them together.

Arrange on a serving platter and drizzle with a good-quality chocolate sauce.

Tessa

During work on Thursday, Tessa decided that she'd pile the cream puffs onto a large red cake platter, with a few strawberries scattered around for a bit of extra colour for the photos. She'd make such a large stack that when she stood behind them, you'd hardly be able to see her.

Prisha was happy when Tessa told her about the upcoming photo shoot for her website. She agreed with Chris about Tessa being in the photos.

"Your products are wonderful. You're wonderful. You want your customers to see that."

Tessa looked over at the shelf holding her jars and bottles of sauces. She remembered how proud she'd been when she'd first seen them there. Everyone she'd ever given them to had raved about how delicious they were. Customers came in for repeat orders and they were one of their most popular gifts and one of the shop's best sellers.

"They are pretty, aren't they?" she said.

Prisha gave her a quick side hug. "I'm proud of you. Don't ever forget how far you've come already."

...

When she got home that afternoon she got to work baking. Abigail had texted to say she'd gone to her dad's but hadn't forgotten about Vanda's event and would be home early on Saturday. Thomas was doing a couple of long shifts at the restaurant so he could have the Saturday night off. Tessa completely lost track of time and had forgotten about dinner, but when she finished that night she had three large plastic containers of cream puffs. She cooked herself a poached egg and went to bed.

...

On Friday morning, Tessa felt nervous about that afternoon, although Prisha did her best to remind her that it was just a photo shoot.

"You don't have to choose any of the photos if you don't like them. Or you could choose one without you in it. The final decision is up to you, right? You might as well give it a shot though."

"That's true." Tessa was tidying up the gift wrap and ribbons. "That actually makes me feel a lot better."

"Wear a skirt and that nice green silk top though, just in case," Prisha added.

She'd allowed plenty of time before Chris arrived to get ready, giving the immaculate kitchen a final wipe over and de-stemming the strawberries with the fancy little gadget her mother had bought her the previous Christmas. She put her hair up into a bun to shower, as she didn't want to have to dry it. Tessa tried not to think about the comment Chris had made as she rubbed her Ecoya lotion into her skin, then dressed and put on some make-up.

By the time Chris was due to arrive, the cream puffs were filled and arranged on the platter and she'd been pacing a track across the kitchen tiles for a good fifteen minutes. He arrived promptly, but not on his bike this time. Chris unloaded tripods, a ring light and something that looked like a white umbrella from a tiny but new-looking Toyota Vitz. He piled everything onto the front step, then went back for his photography bag before ringing the bell.

"Hi, Tessa, nice to see you again," he said.

"Can I give you a hand to bring your gear in?"

They brought everything into the kitchen and Chris looked around. He seemed very professional and Tessa decided she'd imagined the flirting the first time around. Today he was wearing black trousers and a black polo shirt. After he surveyed the kitchen he turned to her and looked her over.

"You look gorgeous," he said. "Perfect choice of outfit."

"I've set up the cream puffs on a platter but I haven't poured the chocolate sauce on yet. I wasn't sure whether I'd chosen the right plate, or where you'd want me, or them or

..." Tessa stopped talking abruptly, aware she was rambling.

"They look luscious." Chris walked over and crouched down to bench level to look at the pastries. His trousers tightened across his arse. When he straightened again, Tessa looked away. Chris was being completely professional, but she wasn't.

"I'll set up then, shall I? We'll leave it until we're ready to pour the sauce over so it drips the right way."

He unpacked his camera bag and placed his equipment around the kitchen, checking out angles and changing things around. He looked up at her from the bench and gave her a smile. "I wouldn't mind a cup of tea, if it's not too much trouble. I came straight from work and didn't have time earlier."

"Of course. Sorry, I should have asked." Tessa was glad to have something to do. Her fingers fumbled over the tea caddy and then she knocked the strawberry stem remover, which skittered across the bench and landed on the floor with a clatter. Chris glanced up at the noise, then down at the floor. His face broke into a grin. "Is that a vibrator?"

"Oh my Lord," Tessa gasped. It did kind of look like a bullet vibe, with its pointed metal end and latex strawberry middle. The top was meant to be the green stem of the strawberry, but could easily be a handle. "No, this is embarrassing, I'm so sorry."

"What are you sorry for?" Chris said. "There's no rule that says you have to use your sex toys in the bedroom."

He was still grinning. It looked as though he was trying

not to laugh. "Unless ... I wasn't clear. It's not *that* kind of photo shoot."

"It's not actually ... it's to de-stem strawberries. I've never had ..."

There was a beat of silence, then Chris laughed. "I'm sorry, that was inappropriate," he said. But he was still smiling. "I'll try to keep things strictly professional."

"So I take it you want me to keep my clothes on?" she asked. She was smiling now too.

"Yes. For now, anyway."

Tessa felt her heart do a little jump now that the flirty tone was back.

"So, chocolate sauce," Chris said.

"Um, pardon?" Tessa squeaked.

"For the cream puffs?"

"Yes, right." She handed him the bottle. "Would you like to do the pouring?"

Chris uncapped the bottle and slowly poured the sauce onto the platter. He was very intent and the way the sauce pooled and dripped was very sensual. He took photos from several angles, fiddling with filters and settings before indicating to Tessa to move in behind the bench. He snapped, moved her around and snapped some more.

"I think that's about it," he said after a while. He eyed the platter. "That sauce looks delicious."

The chocolate sauce was the first product Tessa had made professionally and still one of her favourites. She absently dipped her index finger into the sauce and licked it. "It is."

Chris stared at her for a few seconds.

He cleared his throat. "Actually, could you jump up onto the benchtop? That would make a good shot."

Tessa climbed onto the bench and crossed her legs. She dipped her finger into the sauce again. Chris snapped a couple of photos. She picked up a pastry and bit into it. Cream oozed onto her fingers.

Chris carefully put his camera down and took a step towards her. "This is completely unprofessional after all, but that's so sexy." He moved even closer.

"Would you like one?" Tessa asked him. Her voice came out all throaty.

"Yes, please." Chris was staring at her mouth. "This ... it isn't the kind of thing I would usually do. Not just when I'm working but ..."

...

"Me neither." She held out the cream puff and he took a bite. They looked at each other. He swallowed, took a step forward and kissed her. It wasn't the soft gentle kiss she might have expected and Tessa moaned a little. She tried to brace herself against the bench but her right hand went straight into the plate of pastries. They made a soft, farting kind of noise as they collapsed and cream exploded outwards. Chris pulled off her top and pushed her back onto the bench, into the platter. The rich smell of chocolate filled the kitchen, sweet and a little wicked. Tessa had cream in her hair and she could feel sticky chocolate sauce on the back of her shoulders. There was a smear of chocolate on the side of Chris's face in the shape of a handprint. Tessa pulled him onto the bench.

* * *

It was dark outside after they'd showered and changed. Chris hadn't fared too badly and had sponged cream and chocolate sauce off his clothes. He'd helped her clean the kitchen and then she'd finally got around to making the cup of tea she'd started earlier.

"Well, thanks," Chris said, setting down his cup. "That was delicious."

It wasn't clear which part of the afternoon he was referring to, or maybe it was the cup of tea. "Sorry to rush off, but I've got somewhere I need to be tomorrow and I'm not very organised. I borrowed my sister's car and she was probably expecting it back a while ago."

"I've got something tomorrow too," Tessa said quickly. She suddenly couldn't wait for him to go.

After he left, she realised the lights were blazing in the kitchen. It was the first time she'd shagged with the lights on in years.

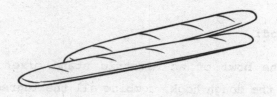

Breadsticks

....

Ingredients:

For the dough:

1 cup + 2 Tbsp warm water

1 1/2 tsp instant yeast

2 Tbsp sugar

3 Tbsp unsalted butter, melted

1 3/4 tsp salt

3 cups bread flour or all-purpose flour

For brushing:

3 Tbsp unsalted butter, melted

1/2 tsp salt

1/4 tsp garlic powder

1/4 tsp Italian seasoning

Method:

In the bowl of an electric stand mixer fitted with the dough hook, combine all the ingredients for the dough except the flour. On low speed, gradually add the flour. Increase the speed to medium and knead the dough for 7 minutes, or until smooth and elastic.

Remove the dough to a lightly oiled bowl and cover with a dry towel. Let it rise in a warm place until it is doubled in size, about 1 1/2 hours.

Divide the dough into 12 portions. Roll each piece of dough into an 18 cm log. Place the dough logs on nonstick baking mats or parchment-lined baking sheets, cover, and let rise until they are doubled in size, about 1 hour.

Preheat the oven to 200℃.

Bake for about 12 minutes, or until golden brown. Meanwhile, combine the butter, salt, garlic powder and Italian seasoning in a small bowl. Remove the breadsticks from the oven and immediately brush with the butter mixture and serve warm.

Tessa

Tessa eyed the silver dress on its hanger.

"Mum!" Abigail shouted from the hallway. "Where's my pink clutch bag?"

"Have you looked on top of your wardrobe?"

Thomas poked his head through the door. He seemed unperturbed to see Tessa standing in her underwear. "Do I need to wear a dress shirt?"

"I'd rather that you did. Gran would like it."

She pulled on the dress and decided it was too late to find something else to wear. They were due at 'The Ferns', a private golf club, in half an hour, and her mother had stressed everyone was to be on time. For whatever this was.

•••

Vanda stood from the table when they arrived, Abigail acting all surly because Tessa hadn't let her drive, and came to hug them all. Brady was already there, sitting next to a woman in a pale-lemon blouse, her hair pulled back in a severe bun.

She was talking quietly to the elderly man next to her who looked to be in his eighties, with a dusting of fine white hair and green eyes.

"I have you next to your brother," Vanda said, tucking in Tessa's bra strap, making her self-conscious about her cleavage. "You look lovely." She seemed nervous. Abigail and Thomas sat at the end of the table and Tessa sat next to her brother while Vanda moved towards an older couple who had arrived. She gave Brady a nudge.

"So what's going on? And where's Mackenzie?"

"We broke up. And Vanda is keeping mum," he shrugged. "She says she'll explain everything when everyone is here." The table was a big one. Set for fourteen. She wondered who 'everyone' was. She didn't recognise any of the people already there and Vanda hadn't introduced any of them.

"Hello," she said across Brady to the others. "I'm Tessa."

"Eleni," said the woman next to Brady. She had a very soft voice. "Howard's ... helper."

The older man turned and gave her a smile. "It's lovely to finally meet you, Tessa," he said. "I'm Howard. I've heard so much about you and your brother from your wonderful mother." He reached over to give her hand a pat. His was warm and age spotted. "Ahh, here's my son, Donald, and his wife, Margot." Vanda came back to the table with the couple who took seats opposite the old man.

"What's this all about then, Dad?" Donald asked, pulling out his chair with a loud scrape on the tiles. He was in a navy pinstripe suit with a silk lavender tie and smelt strongly of cigars. He beckoned a waitress over with an awful finger click and ordered a whisky sour and a gin and tonic with fresh lime. 'Not that awful fake rubbish.'

"All in good time, son," Howard said with a smile. "Let's wait for the grandies, shall we?"

They all ordered a drink except Eleni, who sipped her water and said nothing. Margot glanced around the room, and back at the table. "Gosh, they do take a long time with the service, don't they?" Her voice sounded a little slurry and Tessa wondered if she had maybe had a small stroke, but then the waitress returned with the drinks and Margot drained half of hers in one sitting before ordering another.

"Ah, here they all are," Howard said and they turned collectively to see a group of people enter the dining room, including a small boy of about seven who waved furiously at Howard.

"Holy shite, that's Felicia Bacon," Abigail gasped. "The water polo champion."

"And isn't that Mr Bacon?" Thomas added. "That teacher from school?"

Tess found herself looking at a very familiar face.

* * *

The group spent a few minutes saying hellos and finding seats. Tessa sat trying to compose herself, her face burning. It was definitely Chris. He was in a blazer and white shirt with jeans and he seemed as flustered by the whole thing as she was. She couldn't believe she had had sex with one of

the teachers from her kids' school. She was fairly certain neither Thomas nor Abigail had taken his class but she was still
mortified. Her kids would be disgusted if they ever found out
what they had done. This was awful. The worst thing that
could possibly happen.

• • •

Howard introduced the others. Felicia, who immediately
suggested they call her Flea; Ben, who was a younger version
of Chris, with more hair and light-brown eyes like Margot;
and then Leanne, who seemed to be the mother of Freddie,
who perched himself on Howard's knee and kissed him on
his cheek before announcing he was 'starving and do they
have chicken nuggets here?'

"How about one of these for now?" Flea called out. "Come
sit next to me, champ." Freddie came around the table,
climbing onto a chair, and Flea handed him a homemade
breadstick from a metal holder on the table.

"Right, well, that's everyone so without further ado, I'll
get straight to the point," Howard said. "But first, let's get
some champagne for the table." Donald did that awful clicking thing again and there was a collective cringe from most
of the table as the waitress came over. She came back with
a tray of flutes and another waiter and the bubbles were
poured. Howard stood carefully, Eleni assisting him, and held
out a hand to Vanda, who joined him. He raised his glass.

"Thank you all for coming," he said. "Because today, Vanda and I are getting married."

Feta and
Watermelon Salad

....

Ingredients:

Dressing:

2 Tbsp extra-virgin olive oil

3 Tbsp lime juice

1/2 garlic clove, minced

1/4 tsp sea salt

For the salad:

5 cups cubed watermelon

1 cup diced cucumber

1/4 cup thinly sliced red onion

1/3 cup crumbled feta cheese

1 avocado, cubed

1/3 cup mint or basil leaves

1/2 jalapeño or serrano pepper, thinly sliced

sea salt

Method:

To make the dressing, in a small bowl, whisk together the olive oil, lime juice, garlic and salt.

Arrange the watermelon, cucumber and red onion on a large plate or platter. Drizzle with half the dressing. Top with the feta, avocado, mint or basil, and jalapeño or serrano pepper, and drizzle with remaining dressing. Season to taste and serve.

Tessa

Thoughts swirled round her head, banging against the sides like a pinball. Her mother was getting married. Again. To Howard, who was the grandfather of the man she had wantonly shagged in a sea of cream and chocolate on her kitchen bench. Would that make them related? Had she shagged a relative? What would that make Chris to her? A nephew? A cousin? This was truly awful.

There was a lot of noise. Donald was protesting loudly and saying things like 'What the hell is going on?' and 'Surely there's no need to get married at your age?' Ben was agreeing, with 'How do you even know this woman?' Felicia was saying 'When did this happen?' and 'Why haven't you said anything before now?' Brady was congratulating Howard like he thought it was marvellous. Margot had finished her champagne and was complaining that she shouldn't have to pour her own refill. Freddie shouted out "Why is everyone making so much noise?"

Across the table she caught Chris's eye. They stared at each other for a few seconds. His eyes roamed down her front, lingered on her cleavage and then he flushed and looked up and away.

"What does this mean legally? Has she signed a pre-nup?" asked Leanne, who was sitting beside Chris, and Chris shrugged. His eyes were fixed on his grandfather as though looking anywhere else wasn't an option.

Howard tapped his knife on his flute and eventually the noise died down.

"Everyone, be quiet and let me speak."

The table went silent. All eyes were on the couple who were now sitting. "Vanda and I met when I took some of Ruth's pieces to be cleaned at the jewellers," he said.

"I work at Jennings," Vanda interjected. Howard gave her a smile.

"Vanda was very helpful to me ..."

"Of course she was," Ben muttered.

"... especially when, after she'd examined it, it turned out that a large amount of the jewellery was, in fact, paste." Howard looked around the table at his family as he announced this, a tone to his voice that had Tessa watching their reactions. They all looked shocked.

"What in the blazes are you talking about?" Donald said, rising half out of his seat. "Mum's jewellery? That can't be right. Some of those pieces are worth a fortune."

"Yes, well. Some of them are no longer. I was intending to

gift them to Felicia, as my only granddaughter. But Vanda very gently informed me that some of the pieces had been altered and the gems were no longer real."

The noise level rose and Margot poured another drink, upending the drained bottle back into the ice bucket while Ben ordered a double whisky from a passing waitress, his face pale. Leanne was frowning, her eyes narrowed.

"In any case, I was rather upset. I know she's been gone over twenty years, but I felt like Ruth was taken from me a little bit more. Vanda was an angel. She comforted me. Took me for a lovely cup of tea down the road from Jennings."

Tessa suddenly wondered who Leanne was then if not one of the grandkids. Howard had said he only had one granddaughter. Ben's wife perhaps?

"In any case, a few days later I went back and asked Vanda if she would like to accompany me to dinner — as a way to say thank you."

"We went to Martinas," Vanda said, mainly to Tessa who had always wanted to go. "It was fabulous."

Howard continued. "We had a lovely time, and we've been courting ever since. So a few weeks ago, I asked Vanda for her hand in marriage and she very kindly said yes."

At the end of the table, Ben muttered something that sounded suspiciously like 'gold digger'.

"But Dad, marriage?" Donald huffed, "Surely that's a bit much, I mean, why not just date the woman?"

Howard gave him a long look and cleared his throat.

"We're Catholic, son. And Catholics do things the proper way. I've always been very clear on that. Marriage is until death do you part, and there's no hanky-panky until you say 'I do'. Now without going into that too much, Vanda and I are waiting for that side of things until the honeymoon."

There were a few horrified faces and a couple of snorts from Brady and Flea. Eleni went bright red and then knocked her cutlery off the table trying to get to her glass.

"We're taking a world cruise. I've always wanted to see ancient ruins and eat fresh coconut," Vanda said in a rush. Tessa suspected she was trying to take the idea of geriatric sex from everyone's mind.

"That will be expensive," Leanne muttered to no one in particular.

"In any case, the wedding is today, and after the nuptials we will all sit down and have a meal together and get to know our new family," Howard said firmly.

Tessa downed her champagne.

• • •

The ceremony was brief. Tessa wondered why they had chosen not to do the service in a church if Howard was so pious but suspected it was to do with her mother's lack of faith.

The couple were married by a minister older than Howard, whose hands shook so much Tessa worried he wouldn't make it through the whole service without passing out. When he pronounced them man and wife, Howard kissed Vanda gently and said, "You've made an old man very happy."

Chris had his camera in the car and he went out to retrieve it, taking some shots of the couple out on the deck with the green fields of the golf course behind them. He asked a waiter to come over, showing him a few things on the camera and then joined them all for a group shot.

"Chris, stand next to your lovely wife," Howard told him. He pointed over at Leanne and Freddie and Tessa's heart took a nosedive, in direct contrast to her champagne that was making a valiant effort to revolt.

He was married.

• • •

They headed back to the table, where Tessa felt like she was on autopilot, a fake smile plastered on her face. The staff served the first course and Tessa ate without tasting the feta and watermelon salad.

"Tessa?" Brady said, and it sounded like he had been calling her name for a while.

"Sorry, what?"

"You okay?"

"Huh? Yes, fine. Why?"

"You ate the flower garnish on your starter."

"Oh, right." She looked down at her plate and realised she'd dropped a piece of avocado onto her lap. It had left a smudgy mark. "I need to use the ladies." She got up as quietly as possible and excused herself without looking over at Chris.

• • •

In the bathroom, she dabbed at the stain with a paper towel and tried not to cry. She took a deep breath and steeled herself. This was her mother's day, and she was happy for her. She was. That part of the day was a bit of a shock. The part where she'd shagged a married man was more so.

It's not that bad, she told herself. You did nothing wrong. You didn't know. It's not on you. But she felt terrible. Of all the people to pick to have hot, steamy sex with — good sex too — why did she have to pick a teacher at her kids' school and a married man and her step bloody nephew or whatever he was now?

• • •

Chris was waiting for her, pacing back and forward and chewing on his thumbnail when she came out.

"Tessa, I'm not married," he said the minute she came out the door. "I know what it looks like, but I swear to you, Leanne and I are not together." Tessa waited, not sure what to think.

"Then why did Howard say that?"

"He thinks we are. I haven't gotten up the courage to tell him we split up. He's so adamant with his Catholic upbringing that divorce is a sin, and honestly, Tessa, he means the world to me, that old bloke. You've met my parents. He's my favourite person in our whole family. Except maybe Flea but

..."

"When?" Tessa asked. Chris stopped rambling and looked at her.

"Sorry?"

"When did you split up?"

"Right. God, this is embarrassing. Umm, a year ago? Actually fourteen months now. I know how pathetic that seems, I do. But Howard hadn't been well — we all thought he was on his way out and I couldn't do it. I couldn't tell him. And then it kind of became easier to let him think we were still together. God, I sound like a total coward, don't I?"

"Actually yes, a bit," Tessa said, but she was sort of trying not to smile. He was so earnest and cute and she felt relieved.

"The thing is I bloody fancy you, Tessa, and I'm worried I've totally blown it now."

She wasn't sure why she did it — she blamed the three glasses of champagne — but Tessa leant in and kissed him. It was supposed to be a quick peck, but then they were full on snogging, his hand cupping her arse and her clutching his shirt and his lips devouring her, when a tiny voice below them said, "Dad. Why are you kissing my new granny's daughter?"

Hot and Dirty

....

Ingredients:

45 ml vodka

45 ml gin

splash of olive brine

splash of dry vermouth (optional)

cayenne pepper

olive

Garbanzo/olive foam:

1 part garbanzo bean water

1 part olive brine

Method:

Prepare foam by combining garbanzo bean water and olive brine. Whisk until it creates a foam. Set aside.

Combine vodka, gin and olive brine in a shaker with ice and shake well.

Chill serving glass with ice and a splash of dry vermouth, if using.

Empty glass and strain mixture in.

Top with foam and garnish with cayenne pepper and an olive.

DRINK RESPONSIBLY!

Tessa

Tessa took a step away from Chris and stared down at the little boy, then she turned and bolted down the hall. She could see Brady sitting alone across the room and headed towards him. Halfway there she was intercepted by her mother.

"Tessa, darling, you should try one of these." She handed Tessa a martini glass. "And I need to have a talk with you." Tessa took a large swig. It was rather good, she had to admit.

"Yes, you do. What were you thinking springing something like this on us?"

"I'm sorry, darling, that it was such a shock. I do have to say, I'm not sorry for marrying Howard but I wish I could have told you. Howard wanted to keep it secret from his family, and I respect his reasons, I do. There would have been a bit of an uproar, as you can tell."

"You could have told *us* though."

Vanda laid a hand on Tessa's arm, patting her gently. It was the first time she'd noticed her mother's wedding ring, a gold band inset with four large diamonds. "Yes, I probably could have. But this was our decision. Mine and Howard's. No offence, darling, but it was nothing to do with you."

"Pretty big decision, getting married." Tessa knew she sounded like a sullen teenager.

"I promise next time I'll let you know." Vanda laughed and drained the rest of her cocktail. "I'm off to find another of these and I suggest you do the same. They're delicious, aren't they?"

Tessa watched Vanda walk away with a jaunty hip-sway, resplendent in a pale-blue silk suit and went to join her brother.

"What the hell?" Tessa slid into the seat across from Brady. "Can you believe this?"

"I know." Brady grinned and waved a hand towards the dance floor. "Old Howie's daughter-in-law is off her face."

Tessa looked over to see Margot dancing with a man who was definitely not her husband. She had a cocktail glass in one hand and her hair was slipping from its perfect chignon. Anyone within close proximity was giving her a wide berth as she stumbled around the dance floor.

"Not that, this whole thing."

"Calm down, Tess. Mum's a big girl, she knows what she's doing. Why are you so riled about it?"

Tessa leaned closer to hiss in his ear. "Because I slept with Mum's new grandson."

"You what?" The way Brady jerked upright would have

been amusing if Tessa wasn't feeling so irked.

"Howard's grandson. He's a photographer and he's doing some photos for my website."

"The sleazy-looking guy in the blue suit? Isn't he a bit young for you?"

They both looked over at the dance floor again where Ben was staggering and whooping with his hands in the air.

"That's rich, coming from you. Not that one. Chris. The one with the wife and kid I didn't know he had."

Brady grinned widely. "Ooh. Naughty Tess. Shagging the married relatives. Is that even allowed?"

"Shut up. He says he's not *married* married. Apparently they're not together. Also, he's not really a relative. Is he?"

"So, what is he? Let me think … Mum's grandson?"

"Step-grandson."

"Surely that's a technicality though? But still, brilliant." Brady banged one of his big, meaty hands down on the table and threw his head back, laughing as though it was the funniest thing he'd ever heard.

The music changed and Beyonce's 'Single Ladies' rang out. Margot sidled up to her dance partner, shimmying her hips at him. Donald appeared, striding across the dance floor. He gripped Margot's elbow and led her firmly away.

Ben was at the bar. "A round of shots for everyone!" he shouted, knocking over one of the bar stools with a clatter. Chris was talking to his grandfather and he went over to say something to his brother who shook his hand off his shoulder and turned to talk to the bartender.

"Let me apologise for my family. You must be wondering what you've got yourselves into." Chris's sister, Flea, pulled out a chair and plopped down next to them. "Brady and Tessa, isn't it?"

"Brady Thorpe. I've done commentary on some of your games. You're a real legend."

"Was," Flea laughed. "These days I do less swimming and more designing leisurewear. Not so many early mornings in the pool, which I'm okay with." Abigail had slunk over and was hovering near the table, mouth slightly agape. "My daughter, Abigail, is a huge fan." Tessa beckoned her over and put an arm around her waist. For once, Abigail didn't wriggle away from the contact.

"Do you play?" Flea asked.

Abigail nodded. "I'm in my school's team."

"She's pretty good," Brady said. "She plays centre forward, so a setter, like you were."

"I thought you looked like an athlete. You're strong and muscled and have wonderful posture." She smiled and patted the chair next to her. "Come and sit down and talk to me."

"Really?" Abigail rushed around to sit next to Flea. "I knew you were Mr Bacon's sister but I didn't know we'd end up being related. My best friend, Maddy, is in his art class at school."

"Mr Bacon is a teacher at your school?" Brady let out a

loud cackle. "Gold." Tessa kicked him under the table.

"I want to be a professional water polo player like you," Abigail said.

"Did you know, Chris and I both wanted to join the police force when we were kids? Clearly, with our surname, that would have been a terrible idea."

"Ha, Crispy Bacon," Brady laughed.

"Have you had a chance to meet Chris?" Flea asked.

"Oh yes, we've all met." Brady snorted. Tessa kicked him again. "You know him quite well, don't you, Tessa?"

Flea looked expectantly at her.

"He's doing some photos for my website." She had been thinking she'd tell Chris she couldn't use him any more. That she'd find someone else. Now that she'd blurted it out to everyone, it would seem suspicious if she did that.

This was a disaster in so many different ways.

Loukoumades
(Greek doughnuts)

Ingredients:

240 ml lukewarm water

2 Tbsp sugar

15 g active dry yeast

240 ml lukewarm milk

450 g flour

1 level tsp salt

4 Tbsp olive oil

vegetable oil for frying

To garnish:

350 ml honey

cinnamon powder

chopped walnuts

Method:

Start by making the dough. In a bowl, add the water, sugar and yeast. Stir with a whisk until the yeast dissolves completely and wait for 5 minutes.

In a mixing bowl, add the yeast mixture and the rest of the ingredients for the dough and whisk at high speed for about 2 minutes until the mixture becomes a smooth batter. (You could also use a hand whisk. Whisk until the mixture has no lumps.)

Cover the bowl with some plastic wrap and let the dough rest in a warm place for at least 1 hour to rise.

Into a medium-sized frying pan, pour enough vegetable oil to deep-fry the loukoumades. Heat the oil on a medium heat until hot. Test if the oil is hot enough by dipping in some of the dough for the loukoumades. If it sizzles, the oil is ready. A more accurate way is to use a kitchen thermometer. The oil should be at 160°C.

Dip a tablespoon in some oil, shake it a bit to remove any excess. It is best to dip the spoon in oil and not water. Dip your hand in the dough and using your palm, squeeze out a small portion of dough between your thumb and index finger, like you are making a fist. Using the spoon, grab the dough ball off your hand and let it drop into the hot oil. Repeat this procedure until the surface of the pan is comfortably filled. You should dip the spoon in the oil and shake off every time, so that the batter doesn't stick to it.

While the loukoumades are frying, use a slotted spoon to push them into the oil and turn them on all sides until golden brown. When done, place the loukoumades on kitchen paper to remove the excess oil. Repeat with the rest of the dough.

Then serve on a large platter, drizzled with honey and sprinkled with cinnamon and chopped walnuts.

Eleni

Cora had on her 'race day' hat when Eleni arrived with her Tupperware container in hand. She was dancing in the communal lounge, a blush-pink nightie over the top of a pair of slacks and a long-sleeved singlet. A shopping bag was flung over one arm, stuffed full of random items from her room. Cora had never been to the races, but the hat was an old favourite from a cousin's wedding that she refused to give up. Eleni sighed. The hat was a sign that she was having a very muddled day.

"Good morning, Eleni," a nurse called from the dining room where he was setting up for morning tea. "You look nice."

"Morning, Alan," she called back, looking down at her dress. It was an old comfortable one that she'd had for years with pale roses on the material. The dress had been bought for the same wedding as her mother's hat, she realised. Almost ten years ago. She'd had to replace the buttons on it after Theo managed to pop the three middle ones off while they were sitting at the table at the reception. He'd eaten two of them before she'd even realised. It had been a disaster of a day. She'd had to borrow a man's cufflinks to secure her dress where it kept flapping open and showing her knickers, and then they'd had to take Theo for an X-ray to make sure he was okay. It took two days for the buttons to emerge and Savvas had suggested she wash them and sew them back on. She hadn't.

"I never promised you a rose garden," her mother warbled, coming over to swish the bottom of her dress.

It was tricky to gauge her mother's mood and whether she would recognise Eleni from day to day. If Eleni called her 'Mamá' when she was having a bad day, it tended to make things worse.

"Hello, Cora," she said instead. "I made you some loukoumades."

"My mamá made loukoumades," Cora told her. "If I was a very good girl. Have I been good?" she said in a vague child-like voice.

"You have." Eleni took her mother's elbow and tried to steer her into a chair, but her mother pulled away.

"Don't touch me. I know you killed her. You killed that woman. And Howard. Howard too. Dead."

Alan came over to help.

"Now, Cora, why don't we sit down and have a nice cup of tea?" He pointed towards the dining tables. "A hat like that deserves a fancy cup and saucer I think, don't you?" He gave Eleni a warm smile. He was such a nice man with very kind eyes.

"Thank you, Alan," Eleni murmured, still a little ruffled by her mother's outburst. It was hard to tell if she had been referring to anything real. Of course, Eleni's mind had gone straight to Mrs Beston. But the comment about Howard was odd.

When Eleni was twelve, her yaya Sybil had told her that she would have the 'eye'. She claimed to be a seer and that the gift would skip Cora and go to Eleni. Since Cora had developed dementia, she seemed to have convinced herself that she was clairvoyant like her mother had claimed to be. Most of the time, Eleni was not a believer. Sybil had told her she would be a great healer, which was maybe why she had become a nurse in the first place. But she had also said she would have many children and she saw travel and money in her future. Eleni had only had Tobias and Theo and barely even left her town, never mind the country.

She sank down wearily onto a seat at the table and placed the container on the top.

"Are they your amazing loukoumades?" Alan asked, and Eleni nodded. "Cora, look, your favourite. Let me get you a plate and that cup of tea."

"Please, help yourself too. And the rest of the residents. I made plenty."

"I won't say no to that," Alan said, going over to set the

container on the tea trolley and placing a handful of the doughnuts onto a side plate before bringing it back to the table with Cora's tea. Then he went back to fetch two more. "Milk, no sugar, if I remember right?" He sat down, setting a cup in front of Eleni. "I'm supposed to be on my break, but we're short-staffed today so I might join you ladies, if you don't mind?" He had a cup of tea himself, and he helped himself to a doughnut, popping it into his mouth whole and chewing enthusiastically.

"My God, these are amazing. I'd love the recipe."

"For your wife?" Eleni asked, curious about who Alan might have at home. He grinned. "No wife, just me. And I love to cook." Eleni was surprised. She didn't know many men who cooked. Howard and her father never had and Savvas certainly didn't. 'Women's work', he called it.

"No Theo today?" Alan asked.

"No, he wasn't very keen on coming today. He's at home watching YouTube videos of sea turtles. They're his latest thing."

"How are things going there?" Alan asked. "It's just that you seem tired. Are you getting some respite? Because I know a lady — Barbara is her name — and I think she would be a perfect fit for you."

"I don't know. Savvas doesn't think we need it," Eleni said. Even to her own ears she sounded bitter and pathetic.

"Well, he may not," Alan said carefully, "but it wouldn't hurt to meet her, right? You can say no. You're entitled to it. It won't cost you anything. You can't look after everyone else if you're feeling worn out yourself." He put his hand on Eleni's shoulder and gave it a friendly pat. "Think about it anyway."

...

Eleni checked her watch when she left the rest home and decided she had time to do a quick tidy-up at Howard's before she went home. Her mother had decided she needed a nap after morning tea and Eleni hadn't stayed as long as she normally would.

...

She pulled up to Howard's house and parked out front. The house was a grand old lady in a now affluent area and was worth a fortune, but to Eleni it felt more like home than her own house. She opened the gate and headed up the steps, the sweet scent of roses in the air and she breathed it in, feeling her shoulders relax.

There wasn't much to do. Howard and Vanda had left for their honeymoon the night before and she had done a thorough clean on Thursday, so she just needed to empty the fridge and strip the sheets — she would put new ones on the day before they get back. She gave the kitchen bench a quick wipe down and unloaded the dishwasher, then headed into the bathroom to give it a quick tidy and get the towels.

It was there that she found Howard's fancy brown leather toiletry bag. He'd left it on the counter top. His electric toothbrush, round comb and soft bristle shaving brush were sitting beside it. Inside the bag were all his medications. Including his pills. For his heart.

Howard had not been a well man in recent years. He'd suffered a small stroke and they had found some damage to his heart, put in stents and warned him that at his age, he needed to take it easy.

Eleni held the bottle of pills in her hand and tried frantically to think. Had she forgotten to put the bag into his suitcase? How long ago had he taken his last pill?

What if he died? Her mother's odd prediction ran through her head. What if Howard died? It would be all her fault! She dropped to her knees and prayed.

Abigail

Gran got married. How rando is that? And the guy, Howard, is really old too. Like, older than her. They didn't tell anyone and now they've taken off on a honeymoon on a cruise all over the place. I don't know where.

And not only that but Howard's grandkids are Felicia Bacon and Mr Bacon from school. The Felicia thing is cool. Flea. She's so dope and totally slays at water polo. I got to talk to her about it and we had photos so I put one on my Insta, which is cool. She's literally my idol. I tell Maddy at school and she says I should try to get tickets to the water polo champs. Even though Flea doesn't play competitively any more, she probably still has connections.

It's lunch so we roll up our skirts and sit outside to try to tan our legs. I eat my tub of hummus and some carrot sticks and try to think about how I'm going to look in summer so I can ignore how I still feel hungry. Tiff walks past eating a sausage roll and Maddy does this loud snort.

"Cankles," she says under her breath, and Emily and Jade,

who we are sitting with, laugh. Tiff gives her the finger.

"You've already peaked, Maddy," Tiff says, but she's gone red.

"You'd know, lard-arse!" Maddy yells. I feel kind of mean and a bit bad for Tiff, so I pretend I'm looking for my sunscreen in my bag.

...

I'm glad I don't have Mr Bacon at school. Levi and Maddy do. Maddy thinks he's fine. He's, like, almost bald though. She says all the girls flirt with him. He rides a bike to school and Maddy says he has good legs. Personally, I think Mr Vosper the science teacher is way hotter, but I haven't told Maddy that or she would totally say something to embarrass me.

...

Sucks that Gran is away now though, because I literally need the driving lessons. I want to get my restricted before Maddy does since she isn't seventeen yet so I'm heaps older than her. It will be, like, so cringe if she gets hers first. She reckons she would have already got it if she had more time for driving lessons, but I don't know if that's true. I wish I hadn't told her I was sitting it the second time because she told the whole team when I failed and it was so embarrassing.

Thomas is such an egg. This morning he told me that I had a better chance of getting a licence out of a cereal box than passing, with the way I parallel park. I wish I was an only child like Maddy. Or I had a sister instead of a brother. Gran says we will be like way better friends when we get older, like Mum and Brady, but I can't imagine it.

•••

Brady is taking us to the women's rugby this weekend, which will be cool. He says he might be able to get us a meet and greet with Ruby Tui — pretty dope. Maddy thinks men's rugby is way better but she just likes to perve at the players. The women's team are literally fire. They have serious skills. Even Brady agrees. I think he has the hots for one of the forwards too.

•••

I felt a bit sick and faint at practice yesterday. Coach told me to eat something carby before the game on Sunday, which I don't want to do. I ate a whole bag of vege chips last night after dinner and I was so mad at myself. I literally felt like a total pig after. I have to have more willpower.

•••

Mum is taking me to the game this weekend since Gran's gone. At least she just sits and watches. Dad is a bit embarrassing sometimes when he yells things out. It's not like we can hear him in the water, and he doesn't even know all the rules. Mum just talks to all the other mums and gets coffee.

••••

I ring Maddy and we talk about school for a bit.

"I think I might get my nipples pierced," she says. I think she wants to do it so guys can see them through her togs. "I might get a tattoo as well."

"But in the team rules it says we have to cover up any tattoos and stuff, so what would be the point?"

"God, you're so dry, Abs."

"Well, Coach has a fit if we don't wear our blazers on the bus, so he's not going to let us have anything like a tattoo, is he?"

"I don't care. He can't stop me. I'm going to get a devil on my ankle."

A devil seems a bit lame to me. I'm going to get a New Zealand silver fern or the Olympic rings when I'm a professional athlete representing the country. But I say, "That would be cool."

I look out my bedroom window and I can see Levi's window from mine. Their house is similar to ours, built about forty years ago and old as fuck. Sonya and Alofa give about as much of a shit as my mum does about decorating and trying to make things look nice.

When Levi and I were younger we used to try to do signals to each other and we even tried to string up a pulley system between our houses so we could swap notes, but it got caught in the trees and then Dad cut it down when he did some pruning.

I think about texting him, like 'sup' or something. Maddy is still talking but I kind of forget to listen. So I agree and then say I have to go.

"Okay, but don't forget, if you see Levi, ask him if he thinks I'm hot, yeah?"

"Umm, yeah, maybe."

"He does, I'm sure. I bet he's good in bed too."

I want to ask Maddy who she has slept with but I don't. I haven't done it with anyone yet and she is always going on about sex but I don't know who she has done it with. Also, I hope she doesn't use Levi. He's a pretty good guy.

"Also, can your mum pick me up for the game again? My mum's working."

Maddy's mum is always working. Her dad never takes her to games either. Maddy says he plays golf in the weekend.

"I literally have to go. Laters," she says.

Better than Mickey's
Burger Sauce

....

Ingredients:

3/4 cup whole-egg mayonnaise

1 Tbsp American yellow mustard

2 Tbsp ketchup

2 tsp sriracha sauce

2 Tbsp sweet gherkins, finely chopped

2 tsp gherkin juice

2 tsp white sugar

1/2 tsp white wine vinegar

1/2 tsp paprika

1/2 tsp garlic powder

1/2 tsp onion powder

Method:

Combine all ingredients in a small bowl or jug
and stir until smooth.

Tessa

Early Sunday morning Tessa found herself at the side of the pool sipping a coffee, the smell of chlorine wafting up her nose and the unwelcome chatter of Sally Kemp in her ear. The games were mostly Saturdays with only the odd Sunday one thrown in and normally Keith or Vanda would take Abigail, but Racquel insisted Sundays were their family day and Vanda was on honeymoon. Tessa usually worked on her products in the weekends while the house was quiet, and she felt a little guilty that it had been so long since she had come to a game. Especially because Sally kept helpfully reminding her of this fact.

"I said to Coach Baker only last week that I was starting to wonder if I'd dreamt you up, it's been so long," she said with a horsey laugh. "I'm here every week, of course. Danika got her licence ages ago, so she drives herself to practice, but I still like to come for the games and support the team. It's important to be there for them consistently, don't you think?"

Tessa made a murmuring noise, which Sally seemed to take as agreement.

"A shame Abigail failed her licence, twice now, is it? Poor girl, she must have been so mortified."

"Lots of people take a few goes to get it," Tessa said, then wished she hadn't. It only encouraged Sally.

"Do they? Danika got hers first pop."

"Of course she did."

"How have things been anyway? Are you coping okay on your own?" She gave Tessa a sympathetic look.

Honestly, this woman was so irritating. It wasn't like she and Keith had recently broken up. It was years ago. Tessa knew she shouldn't do it, but she couldn't help herself.

"Absolutely fine, thanks, Sally, how about you? I heard you and Peter had to cut your holiday short a while back when Danika had a bit of a party?"

Sally's toothy smile faded. "No, no, merely a small gathering that got a little out of hand. Gatecrashers, we believe. We were coming back the next day in any case."

"Really? I thought I heard something about the police getting called and confiscating some kegs? Keith said something about replanting your hedge after it was destroyed. Sounded like quite a rager."

That shut her up for a few minutes and Tessa tried to concentrate on the game. The truth was, though, water polo might be fun to play, but it wasn't the most engrossing thing to watch. The players all looked the same in their matching costumes and caps and the whistle seemed to blow constantly for 'contact'. Plus the air was humid and soupy and she was convinced her hair would smell like bleach later.

Tessa's attention kept getting drawn back to the whole drama with Chris. Mr Bacon. He'd texted her several times, suggesting the teacher thing wasn't an issue and asking if they could have dinner, but Tessa was too conflicted to reply. Besides, even if her kids didn't care about her sleeping with a teacher from school, there was still the fact that her mother had married a member of his family. No, she would have to decline. It was a shame that she couldn't think of a way to get out of the photo shoot for her 'Better than Mickey's Burger Sauce' on Friday. And that she couldn't stop thinking about the sex.

• • •

Abigail drove home, Tessa clutching the arm rest and trying to sound calm as she pointed out hazards Abigail seemed oblivious to. They dropped Maddy off first, the car pulling up behind her mother's Mercedes a little too closely for Tessa's peace of mind.

Maddy lived in a beautiful modern contemporary house with wide wrap-around decks and a lap pool down one side. Her mother was out on the second-storey balcony dressed in a pale suit and talking on her phone. She gave Tessa a small, distracted wave and turned away. Tessa had only spoken to her a handful of times and it was usually water polo related.

"I thought your mum was showing an open house today?" Abigail said, and Maddy shrugged. "She'll probably go out again soon. She's always working." She got out of the car with her gear bag, waved goodbye and walked up the immaculately tidy driveway, already on her phone before she reached the door.

"I wish we had a nice house like Maddy's," Abigail complained as she reversed out onto the street, missing the letterbox by mere centimetres. "Ours is such a dump. The only nice bit is the kitchen and that was for you."

"It's not that much of a hovel," Tessa said a little defensively. Yes, their house was older, and a bit cluttered. Sure, the bathrooms were an awful avocado colour from the eighties, but there was nothing wrong with it. Or nothing she could afford to remodel at the moment anyway, and Abigail knew that.

"Mum, my bedroom is Barbie pink," Abigail said scornfully.

"Well, you picked that colour, honey."

"Yeah, when I was seven."

"Well, maybe we can repaint it soon," Tessa said. "Slow down coming up to this pedestrian crossing."

Abigail sighed dramatically and said nothing else until they were driving down their street. "How come we stopped doing the street barbecue?" They drove into the driveway, the car stopping with a jerk. "I was thinking we should do it again."

Tessa glanced at her, surprised. "We haven't done that in years. Not since the Walkers moved out. It was mostly only the three houses anyway. Us, Sonya and Jules. No one else on the street is very social. They were always coming up with reasons not to attend, I seem to remember."

"Still, we could do it with the Taufuas and us? It might be nice."

Tessa looked over at her daughter, fidgeting with the car keys and trying to appear casual. She hid a smile. "Well, sure. Maybe you could have a chat with Levi and see when they might be free."

"Okay, cool. What day?"

"Um, any day but Friday," Tessa said, and then she was back thinking about Chris again.

Koko Alaisa

....

Ingredients:

1 cup short-grained rice

8 cups water

1 can coconut milk or evaporated milk

1/2 cup sugar or to your taste

1 orange leaf or 1 tsp orange peel or a dash of orange extract

1/2 cup Koko Samoa (cocoa powder or grated pure dark chocolate can be substituted)

Method:

In a large pot, combine rice and water. Bring it to a boil. Reduce heat and simmer for 20 minutes. Add milk, sugar and orange leaf or peel and stir until the sugar is dissolved. Add grated Koko Samoa or cocoa to the pot, making sure that the cocoa is fully mixed with the other ingredients. Bring to a boil, stir once more and then remove from the stove top.

Cocoa rice should resemble a thick soup. Serve warm.

Tessa

Chris had turned up for the photo shoot with flowers. Not a big fancy store-bought bunch, but wildflowers that were badly wrapped in baking paper and tied with a rubber band. They were charming. He gave them to Tessa with a smile and went back out the door without a word.

He had his sister's car again, and Thomas had arrived home from work so he helped him unload. Tessa had all the ingredients prepped and the deep-fryer was hot, ready to cook some fries to go with her burgers. She was wearing a simple blue wrap dress and she'd done her hair and make-up in case she had to be in any of the shots, but she was hoping that Chris would only photograph the food this time.

"Thanks, mate," Chris said, putting the last of his equipment down on the dining table and giving her son a smile.

"No prob. I'm gonna head off to bed and catch a few hours of sleep. I'll be up for dinner." Thomas headed up the stairs. It was four in the afternoon, but he'd been on some odd shifts this week and he was good at sleeping any time of the day or night.

Tessa found a jug for the flowers and fiddled with them as Chris set up. She felt awkward around him. There was still a frisson of attraction between them that she was trying hard to ignore.

"I wasn't sure if the burgers needed to be hot or cold, so I precooked a couple of patties," she said. "I have more if we need them hot."

"Cold is fine," he said. "But Tessa, don't you think we should talk?"

"Abigail will be home from *school* soon," Tessa said, placing a strong emphasis on the word 'school'. "So we should probably get going."

"Okay," Chris said quietly.

He set things up and they prepped the burgers, using skewers to give height and a cook's blowtorch to melt the cheese slice just right. Tessa cooked the fries at the last minute so they could get the steam off them in the shot. The sauce was drizzled over the burger patty and in a bowl for the fries and Tessa added some chopped gherkin to the top.

"Do you have cooking spray?" Chris asked. She produced it and he sprayed everything with a thin layer. "Gives it a bit of shine," he told her, positioning lights and getting his camera close to the bench, concentrating on getting the perfect shot. "Would you mind holding the plate up over by the door?" he asked. "The natural light is good." She complied, feeling awkward as he clicked away.

"That colour is great on you," he said. "You look fantastic. Very Nigella." Tessa smiled and he kept snapping pictures for a few minutes, then checked his camera display. "Cool, I think we have what we need," he said. "Were you happy with last week's shots?" He'd emailed them to her earlier in the week.

"Yes, they looked great," Tessa said. "Thanks." But all she could think about was the sex. The bloody great sex right there in this very kitchen.

"Tessa ..." Chris said, only to be interrupted by Abigail bursting through the door with Maddy.

"Mum, Levi said Sonya will bring potato salad and koko alaisa tonight, okay?" She stopped suddenly in the doorway, Maddy running into the back of her with a grunt. "Oh umm, hello, Mr Bacon."

"Hi, Abigail. Hello, Madison," Chris said, looking not at all ruffled.

"Mr Bacon is here to take photos. Of my products," she said, far too quickly. Her voice sounded guilty to her own ears, like they had been caught naked instead of standing fully clothed, talking.

"Hiya, Mr Bacon," Maddy drawled. Abigail nudged her and they both giggled, going over to the bench to make iced coffees while Chris began packing up his gear. Tessa picked up the cold food and dumped it in the compost bin, then loaded the dishes into the dishwasher.

"Are we having burgers tonight?" Abigail asked. Tessa nodded. "Cool. Levi loves burgers." Tessa turned to look at her daughter.

"Wait. What?"

"Can Maddy and I have ours with no buns though?" Abigail went on, grabbing some celery sticks and a pot of hummus from the fridge. "We can wrap them in lettuce." Tessa frowned, thinking of her daughter's earlier comment about the potato salad.

"Wait a minute. Why are Sonya and Levi coming over?"

Abigail rolled her eyes. "The street barbecue, Mum, remember? It's tonight."

"Abigail, I told you any night *but* Friday," Tessa said.

"I thought you said to do it Friday." Abigail shrugged. Tessa felt like strangling her for her casual attitude.

"Are you staying for the barbecue, *sir*?" Maddy asked as Chris came back in for another load of gear. He looked a little baffled.

"I'm sure Mr Bacon has other plans," Tessa said. Then she looked at Chris's face. He was looking at her and his face looked crestfallen. "I mean, not that you're not welcome to stay and eat, if you wanted to," she added.

He gave her a small smile. "I'd love to but I have to get the car back to Flea," he said.

"She could come too," Abigail said. "Couldn't she, Mum?"

Tessa was frantically running through a mental checklist in her head of how many burger patties she had in the fridge.

Did she have more fries in the chest freezer? What about beer? She was going to murder Abigail.

"Of course she could," she said. "She's more than welcome." Chris looked at her for what felt like a long time. "Okay, I'll give her a quick call. See if she's free." He took the last of his gear out to the car and Tessa watched him as he talked on the phone, laughing occasionally.

After a few minutes he came back inside. "She'd love to come," he said. "She wants to know what you need her to bring." Tessa opened her mouth to say that it wasn't necessary for her to bring anything, but Chris pulled her to one side and spoke in a low voice. "Abigail has obviously thrown this on you, so you must need things. Please. Let me help you."

His hand was burning like an electric charge up her arm. Tessa felt the crazy urge to say 'Forget dinner, let's go to bed'.

"Some more tomatoes and lettuce would be great," she said instead. "And maybe some beer?"

"On it," he said, sending a text. "She's going to get whatever you need and Uber over. But what can I do to help?"

···

Sonya and Alofa wandered over half an hour later, carrying plates and cooler bags. Levi was already there, hanging with the girls who had put together a charcuterie board that would have taken Tessa ten minutes to assemble, but had taken them forty and had left the kitchen in need of another tidy. She and Chris had prepped the burger stuff and made small talk, and things were starting to feel less tense between them. They were laying out plates and cutlery when her neighbours came in, Sonya laughing at something her husband had said.

"Kissi la'u muli, babe," she said, pushing in front of him with a grin. "Tessa, tell my idiot husband that there is no way socks and sandals are attractive, will you? Ever."

"Yeah, I'm with Sonn on that one, sorry, Alofa." Tessa came round the bench to help relieve them of all their goodies. "Chris, these are my neighbours, Sonya and Alofa. Guys, this is Chris Bacon, my photographer and a teacher at the kids' school."

"You do remember I don't go to school any more, right, Mum?" Thomas said, coming down the stairs looking like a bear out of hibernation. His hair stuck up on one side and he had a mark across his cheek from where he'd obviously slept against his watch. He opened the fridge and helped himself to a beer, yawning widely.

Sonya gave Chris a long up and down perusal as the men shook hands and then gave Tessa a grin, along with a thumbs up.

"Chris, so nice to meet you finally. Tessa has told me a *lot* about you." Tessa glared at her and gave her a discreet scratching her nose middle finger that made Sonya laugh.

"Wine?" Tessa asked, pulling out some glasses. "Beer, Alofa?"

"I took the last one, sorry," Thomas said sheepishly.

"The cavalry is here," a voice said from the doorway. Flea stood holding a shopping bag and a box of beers, a bag of potato chips balanced on the top. "Hi, guys. I'm Flea."

Abigail had shot up from the outdoor table and came in to say hello. She introduced Maddy and Levi to Flea, beaming with excitement. Maddy, for once, was rather subdued. She looked a little awestruck to meet such a well-known sports-woman and was obviously a fan.

After the introductions were done and drinks poured, they all sat outside on the sheltered deck. It was a little cooler that night so Tessa lit the outdoor heater and they picked at the cheese and crackers and talked. It was lovely. Everyone seemed to be getting on well and eventually they cooked up the burgers and ate.

"This sauce is amazing," Flea said, dunking her burger into a pile on her plate.

"Better than Mickey D's," Thomas and Abigail said in unison and then laughed.

"They used to say that as kids," Tessa explained. "The name stuck."

"It is better, isn't it," Chris said. "You're an amazing cook. Thomas, is that where you get your interest from?"

"He just likes to eat," Abigail said snidely.

"I'll eat to that," Flea agreed, adding a pile of fries to her plate.

"But really, your sauces are great," Chris said quietly to

Tessa. "I think you're amazing."

Tessa's face burned. There was an awkward pause where no one seemed to have anything to say. She wondered if the kids had noticed anything between her and Chris.

"The gnomes are looking fantastic," Sonya said, breaking the silence. "I've found you a beauty for your birthday this year."

"Brilliant," Tessa said with a laugh. "Looking forward to it."

"Do you collect them?" Chris asked.

"She does," Sonya said. "They're her pride and joy, aren't they, Tessa?"

"They're certainly a talking point," Chris said with a grin.

He had been warm and funny to everyone, and eventually Tessa had relaxed and started to enjoy herself. Later, they ate warm cocoa rice and ice cream and conned the kids into doing the dishes.

When they left, Flea thanked her several times and gave her a hug. Chris promised to send the photos over asap and suggested they do another shoot the next week. Then he leant over and gently kissed her cheek.

It had turned out to be a great night, but after everyone went home, all Tessa could think about as she lay in bed alone was how nice it would have been to have someone, Chris maybe, here with her.

Avgolemono

Ingredients:

2 Tbsp extra-virgin olive oil

1 medium onion, chopped

1 medium carrot, peeled and chopped

2 celery stalks, chopped

3 cloves garlic, minced

1 litre chicken broth

1 tsp fresh thyme leaves

1 tsp dried oregano

salt

freshly ground black pepper

½ cup white rice

3 cups shredded chicken

3 large egg yolks

juice of 2 medium lemons

freshly chopped dill, to serve

lemon wedges, to serve

Method:

In a large pot over medium heat, heat the oil. Add onion, carrot and celery and cook until soft, about 5 minutes. Add garlic and cook until fragrant, 1 minute more. Add the broth, thyme and oregano and season with salt and pepper. Bring to the boil. Add rice and reduce heat to a simmer. Simmer until rice is cooked through, about 20 minutes. Add the chicken to the pot and bring it back to a simmer.

In a medium bowl, whisk together the egg yolks and lemon juice. Slowly add ¼ cup of hot broth to the eggs while whisking. Slowly whisk the mixture back into the pot. Let it simmer until thickened, about 5 minutes.

Serve the soup with fresh dill and lemon wedges.

Eleni

Theo was being difficult. He'd woken up that morning and refused to get out of bed.

"Come on, Theo, you've got work today," Eleni pleaded.

"Can't go. I'm sick," Theo said. He'd been perfectly well when he'd gone to bed and had slept pretty well. Eleni felt his forehead and then took his temperature to be sure, but he didn't have a fever.

"How are you sick? What's wrong?" she asked.

"Want to see the turtles."

Eleni sighed. "We can't see turtles, Theo. There are no turtles living here."

"Turtles live at the beach."

"Not here they don't. Come on, up you get, it's a workday today."

"No. Want to see the turtles."

In the end, Eleni rang him in sick to his care centre. As soon as she'd done that, he'd got up and plodded into the kitchen where he'd poured a large bowl of cereal and then overflowed the milk.

It was supermarket day, but she was also sick of the food that got wasted.

Savvas had the TV volume on full and was watching a sports game, a plate of toast balanced on the paunch of his stomach.

"Make me another cup of tea, will ya, while you're in the kitchen?" he called, as she approached him. Even though she was no longer in the kitchen, she turned back and flicked the jug on, unable to deal with him today as well. He'd have thought he was being a massive help to her, making his own toast.

"Theo's off sick," she said as she placed the cup on a coaster on the little table beside the sofa. "There's nothing wrong with him, he's being stubborn, but you're going to have to watch him while I go to the supermarket."

"Why can't you take him with you?" Savvas hadn't taken his eyes off the TV.

"You know how he is at the supermarket. He'll get stressed and I won't get the shopping done." Savvas didn't know how Theo was. He'd never taken him. Theo couldn't deal with crowds of people and the supermarket was a trigger for him. Last time Eleni had tried to take him he'd thrown an entire shelf of eggs onto the floor because the packaging looked 'too grey' and then he'd lain down and screamed. He'd refused to get up, like a huge, overgrown toddler, and it had taken three security men to remove him. That was over a year ago now and Eleni still drove right past that particular supermarket to go to one further away.

It was also her library day. Every two weeks she allowed herself the luxury of going to the library first to swap her book. She'd stop at the little coffee shop with the lace curtains and have a coffee while she read her new book for half an hour. Half an hour of blissful, uninterrupted peace, and then she'd do the grocery shopping.

Savvas grunted an unintelligible reply and Eleni grabbed her keys. Theo was at the table, shovelling cereal into his mouth. He was watching a turtle documentary on his iPad. "Be good for Dad," she said, giving him a quick kiss on the top of his head.

"Turtles, at the beach," Theo said.

"Yes, enjoy your turtles."

...

While Eleni sipped her coffee, she thought again of Howard. She hoped he was enjoying his honeymoon with Vanda, who seemed like a nice lady. It had been such a shock to find out he was getting married. She'd assumed it was a family lunch and Howard had invited her because either he was kind in that way or he'd wanted her to be there as his carer in case he needed help. It made sense now, him asking about the Viagra tablets. The thought of tablets made Eleni think again about the toilet bag Howard had left behind and his heart pills. Was he taking Viagra without taking his heart pills? What would that do to him, when all the blood rushed to his nether regions? Eleni didn't like to think about it — for several reasons. She wished he'd had a mobile phone so she could call him but he didn't. She hoped Vanda had received her text, but hadn't got a reply. Felicia would probably know how to get hold of him on the boat but Eleni felt paralysed with fear at the thought of admitting she may be the one responsible for not making sure he had his medications. She'd be fired at best, and worst-case scenario, Howard could die and it would be her fault. This time it wouldn't be a close call. Eleni had woken in a cold sweat every night since Howard had left. She needed to pluck up the courage to tell one of the family.

• • •

When she pulled into her street after the supermarket, she was alarmed to see a police car parked outside the house. Eleni's first thought flew back to Howard. They'd come to question her, or maybe even arrest her for neglect, or manslaughter or whatever it was she was going to prison for. Who would look after Theo? Who would visit Cora in the home? Would that nice nurse Alan think she was an unfit daughter? It would be all over the papers no doubt and maybe even on the TV news.

Savvas was standing on the porch, talking to a police officer. He had a jam stain on his T-shirt, she noticed, and his grey hair was sticking up as though he'd been running his hands through it.

"Mrs Vasiliou?"

Eleni clutched a grocery bag to her chest. "Yes?"

"I'm Officer Turner. Your husband has reported your son missing. We were hoping you might have some idea of where he could have gone."

"He bloody wandered off! You shouldn't have left him!" Savvas was yelling.

Eleni felt dread settle somewhere in her gut. "You were meant to be watching him." She turned to the officer. "I was at the supermarket. I can't take him to the supermarket. He had a disability, you see ..."

"It's all right, Mrs Vasiliou, we understand. Is there anywhere you think Theo could have gone?"

"He wanted to see turtles. He's obsessed with them. Maybe to the beach? Or a pond?"

The officer nodded, stepped away and spoke into a radio.

"Should I go and look for him?" Eleni asked her, when she came back over.

"No, it's best if you stay here. He may come back on his own and it would be better if he found you both home. We've got people out looking for him. Is there anyone he could have gone to visit?"

Eleni shook her head. "He's not capable of that. He doesn't know where anyone lives."

"Come inside, maybe have a cup of tea," Officer Turner

suggested kindly.

"Yeah, you're causing a spectacle standing out here where the neighbours can see you," Savvas grumbled. "I could do with a cup of tea."

Numbly, Eleni followed them into the house. Her mind was working overtime, thinking of where Theo could be and how frightened he'd be when he couldn't get back home. She thought of him getting run over crossing the road. The fact he couldn't swim. Someone abducting him, though good luck to them trying to get him into the car against his will.

Officer Turner made tea but Eleni could barely sip hers. Her hands were shaking badly and she was worried she was going to throw up. Savvas chomped his way through a packet of biscuits and every crunch made her want to get up and punch him in the face. She'd never been a violent woman but she was so angry with him. And here he was, acting as though it was all her fault. Getting up, she put away the groceries on autopilot, for something to do.

Another police car pulled up and a male officer got out, helping Theo out. Theo came bounding up the stairs, humming happily as he came inside.

Eleni rushed to him and hugged him, but he brushed her off. "I went in the police car with the bright lights."

"Theo, where did you go? Where have you been?"

"We found him at the beach, ma'am. He said he was looking for turtles."

"You mustn't go off like that, Theo."

"There were no turtles. Can we go see the turtles?"

"Your trousers are all wet. Let's get you changed."

"He was wading in the water when we found him. Luckily, he hadn't gotten too far out. It was quite a job persuading him to come back in."

"Thank you," Eleni said. "He can't swim. What if ... thank you, I'm so sorry to have been such a bother."

"It's no bother. We're glad to have found him safe and well."

She saw the officers off and then took Theo up to get changed. He wanted to go back out straight away and find turtles, but she managed to calm him down with another documentary and several of the plastic sea turtles she'd bought him the week before.

Savvas had gone back to watching TV. "What's for lunch?" he asked.

Eleni bit back everything she wanted to say to him. "I'll make soup," she said instead.

"Do some garlic bread as well. I'd like some garlic bread with it."

As she went to the fridge to take out ingredients, she saw the piece of paper in Alan's neat writing, a magnet holding it to the door. It was the number for Barbara, the home help. Eleni made up her mind, then and there, that things were going to change.

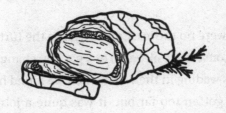

Beef Wellington

....

Ingredients:

a good beef fillet, around 1 kg

3 Tbsp olive oil

250 g mushrooms

50 g butter

large sprig fresh thyme

100 ml dry white wine

12 slices prosciutto

flour for dusting

500 g pack puff pastry, thawed if frozen

2 egg yolks, beaten with 1 tsp water

Method:

Sit the beef fillet on a roasting tray and brush with 1 Tbsp olive oil and season with pepper, then roast for 15 minutes for medium-rare or 20 minutes for medium. When the beef is cooked to your liking, remove from the oven to cool, then chill in the fridge for about 20 minutes.

While the beef is cooling, chop the mushrooms as finely as possible so they have the texture of coarse breadcrumbs.

Heat the rest of the olive oil and the butter in a large pan and fry the mushrooms with the thyme on a medium heat for about 10 minutes, stirring often, until you have a softened mixture.

Season the mushroom mixture, pour the wine over it and cook for about 10 minutes until all the wine has been absorbed. The mixture should hold its shape when stirred.

Remove the mushroom mix from the pan to cool and discard the thyme.

Overlap two pieces of cling film on a large chopping board. Lay the prosciutto on the cling film, slightly overlapping, in a double row.

Spread half the mushroom mix over the prosciutto, then sit the fillet on it and spread the remaining mix over the top.

Use the cling film's edges to draw the prosciutto around the fillet, then roll it into a sausage shape, twisting the ends of cling film to tighten it as you go.

Chill the fillet while you roll out the pastry.

Dust your work surface with a little flour. Roll out a third of the puff pastry to an 18 x 30 cm strip and place on a nonstick baking sheet. Roll out the remainder of the pastry to about 28 x 36 cm.

Unravel the fillet from the cling film and sit it in the centre of the smaller strip of pastry.

Brush the pastry's edges with some of the egg yolk mix, and also the top and sides of the fillet.

Using a rolling pin, carefully lift and drape the larger piece of pastry over the fillet, pressing well into the sides.

Trim the joins to about a 4 cm rim. Seal the rim with the edge of a fork or spoon handle.

Glaze all over with more egg yolk mix and, using the back of a knife, mark the beef Wellington with long diagonal lines taking care not to cut into the pastry.

Chill for at least 30 minutes and up to 24 hours.

Preheat the oven to 220℃.

Brush the Wellington with a little more egg yolk mix and cook until pastry is golden and crisp; 20—25 minutes for medium-rare beef, 30 minutes for medium. Allow to stand for 10 minutes before serving in thick slices.

Tessa

The Instagram page for Taste of Tessa was starting to look great, Tessa had to admit. Her newly updated website too. She had another meeting with Seth to make sure she was happy with what he'd done and he showed her how to upload future pictures herself. Chris had come back the week after the street barbecue and they'd done a block of photos for several of the products and she was happy with how uniform it was looking. Then he'd had to miss a week because of commitments at school and a photo shoot for a new winery and she was surprised to find she'd missed him.

When he turned up early for the next shoot, she was caught off guard. She had dropped Abigail at Keith's last minute — Abigail hadn't been ready when Thomas left for work — and Tessa had been intending to change and put a bit of make-up on before Chris arrived.

As usual, he unloaded his gear into the front porch, knocked and Tessa let him in. This time, however, he was standing holding the ugliest garden gnome Tessa had ever seen. It had a large red bow stuck onto the top of its white chef's hat and an almost manic-looking grimace on its face, like it was going to smash someone in the face with the pie it was holding rather than offer it to them to eat.

"This is for you. I can see you like them and I ... er ... thought you might like one for your collection."

"Wow ... thanks." Tessa took the gnome. It was a rather sweet gesture. One she hoped he wouldn't make a habit of. How could she tell him she hated garden gnomes and they were only to piss off her ex-husband. "I'll put it right by the daphne bush."

Keith would absolutely hate it, at least.

"Sorry I'm a bit early but I was at a loose end and hoped we could get straight into it. What are we shooting today?"

He followed her inside, where she had a large bowl of fresh strawberries sitting on the kitchen counter. This time, she'd made sure to put the stem remover back in the drawer.

"I thought we could do something simple, strawberries with my orange Cointreau sauce, and I've got a beef Wellington in the oven to go with the thyme and wine jus. And maybe something with the meat rub to go along with that." She felt her face heating, ridiculously, when she mentioned the meat rub.

"Strawberries photograph great," Chris said, beginning to set up.

"I, um, thought ..." Tessa folded the apron she'd been wearing earlier and put it on the bench near the stove. "I thought maybe you'd like to stay and eat with me later." He gave her a look she couldn't read. "As friends," she added, feeling awkward all of a sudden.

Chris grinned at her. "A home-cooked meal and great company? Not going to say no to that." He turned back to what he was doing. "Although I think we both know I'd like to be way more than friends, Tessa."

God, she wanted that too. She did. But what about the kids? And her mum? And Howard? But he was standing there in her kitchen and all she wanted to do was go to bed with him. There was such a strong rush of attraction between them, such a magnetic pull towards him. What if they did it one more time? No one would have to know, would they? And she wanted this one thing for herself. Just one more time.

"Bugger it. Let's go upstairs," she said, and Chris did that sexy raising-one-eyebrow thing. "Do you mean ...?"

"Yep."

"Okay then."

She led him up the stairs to her room. Thankfully it was fairly clean and the bed was made. When she got in the door, she turned to look at him. He was walking in behind her, pulling off his T-shirt, looking at her. Her heart started beating in her throat. God, she'd never done this before. Not sex — she'd obviously done that before — but this whole leading a man up to her boudoir thing. She had no idea now how to act or what to do next.

When she'd first met Keith, they'd had a pretty good sex life. They weren't overly adventurous but they did it often. It wasn't until after the children were born and he'd started to suggest she lose a bit of weight and tone up that Tessa had lost all enthusiasm. It didn't help that he never did anything around the house or with the kids. She was always tired. Abigail was a colicky baby and a terrible sleeper. There was invoicing to be done for the business and Tessa did most of the correspondence with customers, following up on quotes and ordering stock. Both children had been fussy eaters and she'd got into the habit of cooking several different meals for them each night, then eating the leftovers as she couldn't bear to throw them away. She'd eat again with Keith when he came home, even though she wasn't hungry. Tessa felt frumpy and shapeless. Keith would admire other women's bodies in public and bemoan the fact that Tessa had been slim when they'd met. He joked that it was 'false advertising' and he didn't know what he was getting. They had sex with the lights out. Keith avoided touching her body except when necessary and eventually they stopped having any intimacy at all.

...

Tessa's last relationship — if you could even call it that — was with Gary, a keen gardener with a foot fetish who had been a regular customer. That had been last summer. They'd gone out a few times and he'd admired her feet in their strappy summer sandals and was overly invested in what colour she was going to paint her toenails. But it had gotten a bit weird and she'd discovered that what he was into wasn't what she was into at all.

Luckily, Gary had moved towns and she didn't have to worry about him lurking in the Outdoor Furniture section any more, hoping to have a chat and furtively eyeballing her toes.

Now, she had made a move, but had no idea how to follow through. Would it be weird if she drew the curtains? Asked him to look away while she undressed and got under the covers? She stood there, feeling like a total fraud, until Chris came over and took her hand.

"What's up? You look like maybe you've changed your mind?" His thumb stroked the back of her hand gently. "It's okay if you have."

"I'm so big," she blurted out. "And you're so lean and toned and ..." He cut her off with a kiss. A long, firm, forceful kiss that made her toes curl, in a good way.

"You're perfect to me," he said.

• • •

After, as they lay in bed, a little sweaty and sated, Tessa realised she had forgotten to worry about her stomach or her bum or the sway of her boobs or any of those things that had made her stop enjoying sex. She had enjoyed it immensely.

"We can't let anyone know," she said after a while. "If we do this, I mean. My kids can't find out. Or Mum, or ... oh shit!"

She leapt out of bed, grabbing at the first thing she could find, threw it on, then took off down the stairs.

"What's wrong?" Chris called from behind her.

"I forgot about the beef Wellington."

. . .

She managed to save it, although one side was slightly over-done. Chris set about photographing it from the good side while she sorted some green beans to go with it. He took some photos of the strawberries as well and then they sat to eat on the bar stools at the counter, finishing off the last of a bottle of Pinot Noir that Tessa had open.

The kitchen was a shambles and Tessa was still wearing the satin floral dressing gown she'd thrown on earlier. It was one the kids had given her for Mother's Day and it was rather short considering what she didn't have on under it. As they ate they kept grinning at each other every time their eyes met and Tessa felt a bit like her teenage daughter.

She got up to start the dishes, bending and pulling out the dirty baking dish from the oven. Behind her, there was a click of the camera.

"You did not take a photo of my arse," she said, looking at Chris who was grinning at her like a schoolboy. He clicked the camera again.

"I did. And you look so bloody good, I may have to stay seated for a little bit while I calm myself down."

Tessa looked over at him. He was into her, she realised. For whatever reason. She took a deep breath.

"Well, maybe I could take care of that for you first," she said, going over to see what all the excitement was about.

Hey Pesto

....

Ingredients:

1 1/2 cups basil

1/2 cup flat-leaf parsley leaves and 1/2 cup stalks

1/2 clove garlic

1/4 cup toasted pine nuts

1/4 cup grated Parmesan

1/3 cup extra-virgin olive oil

1–2 Tbsp lemon juice

salt and black pepper

Method:

Combine basil, flat-leaf parsley (leaves and stalks), garlic, toasted pine nuts and grated Parmesan in a food processor.

With the motor running, slowly add extra-virgin olive oil, then season to taste with lemon juice, salt and black pepper.

Tessa

"I'm moving out," Thomas announced a few weeks later over breakfast. "I'm going to shift on Friday before work."

"Woohoo," Abigail said with a grin. "Can I have your room?"

Tessa poured some granola into her bowl of berries and added Greek yoghurt. She'd been dreading this moment and yet, now that it was here, she wasn't as upset as she'd thought she might be.

Perhaps that was due to Chris. They had been seeing each other once or twice a week and Thomas's schedule had been something of a pain to work around since he was often home at odd hours and his shifts changed every five days or so. Twice they had nearly been caught out and had to make up excuses, but she didn't think Thomas had worked it out.

"Do you need anything?" she asked. "There's a heap of stuff in the garage from the kitchen clear-out that I was going to donate. Do you want to take your linen?"

"I'll have a look through it all tomorrow when I get home from work. Thanks, Mum."

"I'll miss you," Tessa added. "When am I going to see you?"

"I was thinking I could still come over for dinner when Brady does, if I'm not working."

"That sounds perfect, hun." Tessa smiled.

"So can I have his room?" Abigail asked again, spooning yoghurt over her berries.

"Maybe. Do you want granola? It's the apricot one I make." Abigail took a moment to contemplate, then nodded and poured a small amount into her bowl. She put a tiny spoonful into her mouth and swallowed. She'd taken to eating everything with a teaspoon so that the food took longer to eat.

"Dad said the doctor told Racquel she needs to put on weight if she wants another baby," she told them. "He said she needs to exercise less to try to stabilise her cycle and that it might be why she's not conceiving."

"She is pretty skinny," Thomas said, dumping his plate in the sink. "Hurry up if you want a ride to school, Abs. I have to get gas on the way to work so I need to go soon."

"I'm catching the bus," Abigail announced.

"What?" said Tessa and Thomas in unison.

"Since when do you catch the bus? I thought it wasn't 'hip'," Tessa said dubiously.

"No one says 'hip', Mum," Abigail said scathingly, "and heaps of people catch the bus. Levi does."

Ah, things became clearer to Tessa.

"Also, it's good for the environment," Abigail added.

"Okay then, I'm off." Thomas gave Tessa a kiss on the cheek. "Bye, love ya."

"Anyway, when is Gran coming back?" Abigail asked. "Dad is always late picking me up and he won't let me drive his truck."

"Not for another six weeks, I think," Tessa said, finishing off her coffee. "I think they're in Tenerife now. Or maybe Lanzarote. I haven't heard from her much. She says the reception is terrible, so just the odd text message, really."

"Probably having too much fun getting down and dirty on her honeymoon," Abigail said with an evil laugh. Tessa made a vomiting face at her and got up to put the yoghurt and fruit back in the fridge.

"There's Levi now." Abigail stood and touched up her hair. "Gotta go."

Tessa stood in the kitchen and surveyed the mess — Abigail's half-eaten breakfast on the table, Thomas's bowl and cup in the sink — and sighed. Perhaps her kids growing up and moving out was a good thing, she thought, loading up the dishwasher.

...

Chris had come over that afternoon while Abigail was at practice and they had taken some photos of Tessa's pesto sauce, photographing it on a pizza, tossed through pasta and swirled through a soup to show its versatility. Then they'd gone to bed.

They were lying under the covers talking about Vanda and Howard's trip when Chris's phone rang again. It was the third time and he hit the answer button with a resigned sigh.

"Sorry," he mouthed. "Hey, what's up?"

Tessa tried not to listen in, but she was right there and she didn't want to get out of bed. Besides, he was sitting up with his back to her and his back was a lovely muscled expanse of olive skin.

"What do you need it for?" he asked. Then, "How much?" He whistled. "Nah, man, I haven't got that sort of money. No, not spare, I don't. No, nup. Sorry."

When he hung up, he cracked his neck and lay back down in the bed.

"That was Ben," he said, as he rolled towards her, pulling down the sheet a little to expose her breasts slightly. "Mmm. That's better."

"What did he want?"

"The usual. Money." He sighed. "It's always money."

"What does he do again?"

"He's in the family business with Dad. Ladders."

"Ladders?"

"Yep. Bacon Ladders. Howard invented a safety ladder years ago and was smart enough to patent it. Made a fortune in the end. Dad took over and then I was supposed to follow suit. There was a bit of a drama when I said I wanted to teach instead. Dad was not happy. Or Leanne. So Ben's working there now. The plan was for him to take over, but it won't happen."

He inched the sheet down even further, exposing a nipple. It pebbled in the cold air.

"You have great breasts," he said.

"Why won't it happen?" Tessa asked, feeling rather distracted.

"With Ben? He's an addict. Plus I think he's been gambling again. I'm sure that's what he wants the money for. He gets himself into debt and then thinks he can win the money back to pay it off." He tweaked a nipple. "You looked so sexy in that dress at the wedding." He pulled the sheet down further.

"Stop," Tessa said. "You do not want to look at my belly." Chris gave her a long look.

'Tessa, I don't think you get how attractive you are."

"I am not," Tessa protested.

"You are to me. I wish you could see yourself through my eyes." He looked thoughtful. "You know what?" He reached over her to the bedside table where he had put his camera. "I'm going to show you how sexy you look to me."

He scrolled through some photos on the screen and then hit a couple of buttons. "There. Have a look at those pictures I sent you."

"What, now? My phone's downstairs," Tessa said, as she went to sit up.

"In that case, no. Look at them later. I hadn't finished looking myself," he said, ducking under the covers.

It wasn't until later that night that Tessa remembered the images he'd sent. There were several. They were candid shots, most that she hadn't known he'd taken. Some of her in the kitchen, the ones of her in the dressing gown, and one of her taking it off, her back to him and her side profile in view. She had to admit, she looked pretty good. Sexy even. Then again, he was a professional, she told herself. He knew how to make her look good. But she saved the photos to her camera roll, a tiny little voice in her head telling her that maybe, just maybe, she was okay as she was.

Abigail

I'm so glad Thomas is moving out. I might move into his room but mine has a better view so I don't know. I'm doing a deep-conditioning mask on my hair when Levi rings me.

"Hey, did I leave my hoodie at yours?"

I eyeball it on my chair. "Don't think so?"

"Damn. I can't find it. What are you up to? You doing anything this weekend?"

"Dunno. Maddy says there's a party at Dex's house."

"Yeah? Could be keen, I guess. He's a bit of a dick though."

"Maddy kind of went out with him though, so it might be weird." I'm curious to see what he says about that. Maddy has been going on about Levi being hot and into her, so I'm trying to find out if he really likes her. I feel a bit yuk at the thought. I think I might actually like Levi myself. But all the guys like Maddy, not me.

"We could go to the movies?" he says. He sounds pretty chill, so it's hard to tell if he's bummed about Dex or not. "I think the new Marvel movie is out on Thursday."

"Yeah, maybe. I'll see what she says."

"Right. Yeah." I can hear him clicking on his computer and the sound of purring. "I guess I could ask Tyrone if he wants to come too."

"Is that Oti?" I ask. Oti means goat in Samoan. Levi says he called him that because he's the Greatest Of All Time.

"Yeah. He's on my design textbook, so I can't do any work."

"Ha. How random was it having Mr Bacon here the other night?"

"Yeah. He's pretty dope though for a teacher."

"Flea is the best. She said she might come to watch one of my games. Imagine if she does?"

"Yeah, pretty dope." I can hear Sonya yelling something and Levi sighs.

"Hey, I gotta go. Dad pushed the wrong button on the TV remote again and they need me to sort it."

"Okay, cool."

"I'll see you at the bus stop in the morning?"

• • •

After I hang up, I text Maddy to see if she wants to go to the movies instead, but she replies 'Lame'.

• • •

Dad told me a while ago that he and Racquel are trying for another baby. Why did he have to tell me that? Now all I can think of is them having sex, which is gross. But he said the doctor wants Racquel to gain some weight. Which is weird 'cause I thought being skinny would be good. Maybe it's just Dad being too old.

Sometimes, I can hear them in their room and I'm pretty sure they're doing it. Dad makes these gross grunting noises and Racquel does a weird kind of squeak. I'm fully telling myself they are doing more yoga though. Otherwise I will totally need therapy, maybe well into my twenties.

Thank God Mum is too old and boring to have a boyfriend.

Quince Paste

Ingredients:

1 kg peeled and cored quince, diced in 2 cm chunks (weight is after peeling and coring)

3 1/2 cups white granulated sugar

2 Tbsp lemon juice

1 cup water

Method:

Place the diced quince in a medium pot over medium heat along with the sugar, lemon juice and water. Bring the mixture to a simmer, stirring occasionally to melt the sugar.

Continue to simmer over medium heat for an hour or so, stirring occasionally. During this time, the quince will progressively turn into a beautiful ruby-red colour.

Simmer until a candy or instant-read thermometer reads 100℃. This doesn't always guarantee it's ready, so at this point also do a plate test to make sure the mixture is done. Spoon a little of the liquid onto a cold plate and wait a couple of minutes. Push the liquid with your finger and if it wrinkles, it is ready. If it doesn't, continue to simmer and test again.

Grease a 20 x 20 cm glass baking dish.

Puree the mixture with an immersion blender, Vitamix or similar.

Pour the hot mixture into the greased baking dish and use the back of a spoon to smooth the top. Let it cool to room temperature, then cover with plastic wrap and refrigerate for 24—48 hours until firm. Invert the quince paste onto a platter (you may need to gently pry it out with a knife).

Cover with plastic wrap and store in the fridge for up to 3 months or longer. For longer storage, it can be frozen well-wrapped for up to a year.

Serve quince paste with your cheese and charcuterie board. It is traditionally served with manchego but pairs beautifully with most aged, hard cheeses.

You can also cut it into small squares and dehydrate them at a low temperature for a while in the oven to firm them up, then roll them in sugar as a sweet confection.

Tessa

"I should get up and check on my quince paste," Tessa said half-heartedly. She was lying on the couch, clothes in a trail from the kitchen to the lounge floor and Chris draped over her, half asleep.

They were seeing each other secretly. Chris didn't work full days, so he was fairly flexible, whipping over on his bike during lunch and free periods to distract Tessa. They spent a lot of time in bed, getting to know each other's bodies. Often they didn't even make it to the bed. They also did a lot of talking, which was nice too.

"Don't get up," Chris murmured into her neck. "If you give me half an hour, I might be up again." Tessa laughed.

"Maybe when you were a teenager," she said, wriggling out from under him and quickly pulling on her underwear. "That was a hundred years ago for both of us, remember."

"We're not that old." Chris sat up and leaned over the couch, trying to locate his underwear.

"I'm older than you." She pulled on her dress and attempted to fix her sweat-damp hair into something that didn't say 'just been shagged'.

The back door slammed and there were footsteps up the stairs.

"Mum!" Abigail yelled. "Why didn't you remind me to take my photos in for the family history project? I had to get a ride back to pick them up."

"Shit," Tessa hissed under her breath, throwing Chris his shorts and trying to sound normal as she answered. "I did. I left them on the table for you this morning."

Abigail thumped back down the stairs and Tessa grabbed Chris's shirt from where it had been flung over the fruit bowl, turning and wetting it in the sink as her daughter appeared in the kitchen doorway.

"Well, I didn't see them," she told Tessa accusingly. "What are you doing?"

"What? Right, umm, Mr Bacon got some marks on his top when he was photographing things. Food. For my website. On the internet. He takes photos."

Abigail picked up the folder off the table and headed out the door.

"Whatever. I gotta go, Lindsay is waiting for me." She paused, then came back in. Tessa held her breath. "Can I have some money?"

"Sure." Tessa rummaged in her handbag. "Oh, no. I don't have any cash, sorry, hon."

"I'll take your card," Abigail said, swiping it from her wallet and heading out the door. "It smells like something's burning," she called over her shoulder.

"Don't spend too much, Abigail. Do you even know my PIN number?" Tessa called after her, going over to check on the quince paste and finally taking a calming breath. She put the thermometer into the pot, feeling like her face was hotter than the mix inside it.

Chris emerged wearing his shorts, holding his undies, and with a guilty grin on his face. He went over to the sink to retrieve his top.

"Sorry about the wet T-shirt," Tessa said. "I panicked. I wasn't sure if she'd seen your bike outside."

He shrugged. "Want to go on a picnic tomorrow?" he asked her. "We could take some cute photos in the park?"

...

The botanical gardens were full of beautiful autumn colours and Tessa had the cutest wicker picnic basket and red checked tablecloth laid out on the grass, a bountiful mauve hydrangea bush behind them. She had a knife, crackers and two cheeses, her quince paste and grapes spread out on a wooden board as well as two wine flutes filled with a sparkling rosé.

Chris was supposed to be taking pictures of it, but he kept snapping photos of her instead.

"God, that dress looks good on you," he said. "You should

wear it more often."

"You say that about every dress I wear," Tessa said with a laugh.

"Well, dresses are clearly your thing."

"Or yours," Tessa grinned.

"Hello. there," someone said behind her. Chris looked up from his camera, startled.

"Oh, hey, Leanne."

Tessa turned and saw the woman from the wedding. Chris's ex-wife. She was dressed in leggings and a T-shirt and carried a water bottle, her hair up in a short ponytail.

"I thought that was you. Sorry if I'm interrupting your work," she said, eyeing Tessa up and down. "Is your photography thing taking off now?" She did a funny little laugh. "Does it pay any better than teaching at least?"

"Tessa, this is Leanne," Chris said. "Leanne, Tessa."

"I think we met at the wedding, didn't we?" Leanne said. "I'm sure Freddie mentioned something about you."

Tessa's face flamed, thinking about Freddie catching them kissing.

Chris crouched down, snapping pictures of the picnic set-up.

"I need to get this done before the cheese gets sweaty," he said. Tessa wasn't sure if he was talking to her or Leanne.

"I'll see you later then," Leanne said. "I'd better finish my exercise. I had a big lunch and I need to walk it off. We have to watch our figures as we get older, don't we, Tessa?" She patted her upper thigh. "A moment on the lips, a lifetime on the hips." Then she set off down the path.

Chris stood and flicked through his camera screen before putting the screen cap on and tucking it into its bag.

"Right, they look great. Can we eat all this now?" he said, passing her a glass of wine.

. . .

"So you and Leanne get on okay then?" Tessa asked as they drove home.

"Enough to be civil around Freddie, yeah. And so long as we don't talk about much else."

"She doesn't like you teaching much, does she?"

"No. She'd rather I did something more ambitious. She's always been about social standing. And money. The first time I took her round to Grandad's house, she spent the whole ride home talking about how we could move in when he died. She wanted me to join the ladder business more than Dad, I think. Teaching doesn't fit her ideal." Chris pulled a face.

"But you seem good with kids, from what I've seen. And it's so important to have teachers who are passionate about their jobs. Surely that's the most important thing?"

Chris gave her a slow smile. "You wouldn't rather I become a famous photographer? Earning big money and living a glamorous life?"

Tessa pulled up at the lights and gave him a long look. "Is that your dream?"

"No. Photography is a passion, but I love teaching more."

"Well, it sounds like you have the balance just right then."

He leant over and gave her a long kiss until the car behind them tooted that the light was green.

Nuts for You
Peanut Sauce

....

Ingredients:

1/2 cup peanut butter

1/3 cup soy sauce

2 Tbsp sesame oil (toasted or dark)

2—3 Tbsp sugar

small knob of fresh ginger, peeled

clove of fresh garlic, peeled

1/4 cup water

2 Tbsp rice vinegar

2 Tbsp sambal oelek or chilli paste

Method:

Blend all the ingredients together in a small blender or food processor until smooth and creamy. Use it for noodles, rice bowls, grilled chicken, sautéed tofu, in salad dressings or as a dipping sauce.

Tessa

On the weekends when Abigail was at her father's and Chris didn't have Freddie, they would go out for what Tessa had to admit could only be considered dates. Out for dinners, to the movies, for small hikes and even a vineyard. It was rather lovely except for the fact that their families had no idea they were dating.

They had planned to go for a drive to a small beach town and have lunch when Chris rang to say something had come up and he'd needed to swap weekends with Leanne.

"Would you mind if Freddie came with us?" he asked hopefully. Tessa had agreed, feeling oddly nervous. He said he would pick her up and she spent the next ten minutes trying to decide if she should get changed, before realising she was being ridiculous and going outside to wait.

...

Chris pulled up in Flea's car again, Freddie in the back seat perched on his booster. He gave her a funny little wave.

"Hi, guys." She hopped in and pulled the door shut. Chris leant over and gave her a quick kiss on the cheek. He pulled out onto the road, turning down the volume on The Wiggles at the same time.

"I was saying to Freddie that I might need to look at buying a car, wasn't I, mate?" He looked over his shoulder at Freddie and grinned. "Freddie thinks I should get a racing car."

"Or a limousine," Freddie said, making Chris and Tessa laugh.

"I think I might be wearing out my welcome using Flea's all the time," Chris said. "But now I'm doing more photo stuff, the bike isn't cutting it."

"That reminds me, you didn't send through the invoice for last week," Tessa said, rummaging in her bag and pulling out a container. "I made blueberry muffins for the ride. Would you like one, Freddie?" He took one and said thank you.

"Yeah, about that. It feels a bit weird charging you for my services when we're doing what we're doing after," Chris said with a laugh, helping himself to a muffin too.

"Chris, that's crazy," Tessa said, shocked. "Of course I'm going to pay you."

"Well, it's only a part-time thing, and I'm not doing it for the money."

"Still, just because you do something because you love it, doesn't mean you can't get paid. Your photos are beautiful and worth every cent."

"You sound like Leanne," he said, and she frowned.

"I'm not saying it because I think you need to be more ambitious with the photography business, quite the opposite. I don't want to take advantage."

"You can take advantage of me any time you like," he said with a wink.

"Dad?" Freddie asked from the back seat, his mouth full of muffin crumbs. "Is Tessa the one who makes the chocolate sauce that you spilt on your pants?" Tessa looked nervously over at Chris, who was smiling.

"She sure is, mate," Chris said.

"Okay." He stuffed the last bit of muffin into his mouth. "These are yummy muffins. Can I have another one?"

Tessa wished things were that simple with her own children. She didn't like sneaking around as if they were doing something wrong. She missed her mother. She would know what to do. Then she remembered Vanda was on her honeymoon — with Chris's grandfather.

...

Later that evening, she and Sonya sat outside, rugged up in blankets, drank wine and chatted. Alofa was doing a night shift at the hospital where he worked as an orderly and Sonya hated being home alone. The bugs were out in force so they'd turned off the outdoor lights and were sitting with only a candle to light the rice paper rolls and peanut dipping sauce they were having for dinner. Abigail was upstairs with Maddy, music blaring, and Tessa was hoping they would go soon to the party they had spent hours getting ready for. Sonya reached over and took a roll.

"So what's Brady's new girlfriend like?"

Tessa gave her an eye roll. "A carbon copy of all the others," she said. "Tall, blonde, a bit dull. God, that's probably mean, isn't it? I've only met her once. She could have hidden depths."

Sonya laughed. "This is Brady we're talking about. The only thing deep about his partners is their cleavage."

There was a rustle in the bushes to their left and someone emerged from the gate in the hedge, wrapped in something red and blue.

"Abigail!" they shouted. "Will you go out with me?" It wasn't loud enough over the music so they moved slightly to the left, stumbled over a garden gnome and landed on the grass with a 'Fark'.

"Is that ...?" Tessa got up to turn on the light.

"Levi Aleku Taufua, that'd better not be you," Sonya said loudly. "And is that your father's Samoan flag?"

Upstairs, the music stopped abruptly and two heads appeared out of Abigail's bedroom window.

"Oh my gawd," Maddy shrieked. "I knew he fancied me."

Levi pulled himself back onto his feet. "Abigail," he called.

"Levi Taufua, take that flag off. That is very disrespectful," Sonya said sternly.

Levi lifted his hand to wave to Abigail. And dropped the

flag. Underneath he was stark bollocking naked.

Maddy shrieked again.

"Will you go out with me, Abigail?"

"Of course she's not going to go out with you ..." Sonya huffed.

"Yes," Abigail called down.

Levi grinned, picked up the flag and slung it over his shoulders. Then, hobbling a little, he sauntered back through the bushes the way he'd come.

...

Tessa snuck out the next morning while the girls were still sleeping. She was meeting Chris and Flea for brunch, apparently at Flea's request.

"She has something she wants to talk to you about," Chris had said, which had made Tessa nervous until he added, "Nothing about us."

The cafe was a renovated villa on a busy corner site, which would have been a nightmare to live in but was perfect for a restaurant. There were colourful wooden picnic tables and old-fashioned beach umbrellas spread around the front deck extension. When Tessa arrived, she was pleased to see they'd nabbed one of the tables in the sun. Chris and Flea both gave her a hug and she slipped into the seat. Chris slid a menu over. She gave it a quick read, her stomach rumbling.

"The fruit bowl sounds good," she said and Chris stood. "I'll get it, coffee too?"

"Yes, thanks." Should she offer to pay, she wondered.

"I'll get the veggie brekkie with bacon and an oat flat white." Flea handed him her menu. "Also a Green Goddess smoothie and a piece of ginger slice."

"Don't ask for much," Chris grumbled, but then he gave her a grin and made his way inside to order.

"So," Flea said, pushing her oversized sunnies up into her hair. "I have a favour to ask. Actually, it's more a favour of Abigail, but I wanted to run it by you first to make sure you'd be good with it."

"Okay?"

"My next season's line of sportswear is focusing on children and younger women, but *real* women, with realistic body shapes. We want to do a photo shoot in fun locations, showing people being active and confident. I'm not sure whether Abigail would be interested or not, but she'd be perfect. I didn't want to ask her if it was something you wouldn't want her doing."

"She's never done any modelling before," Tessa said.

"That's not so important. She plays sports, she's used to being given direction and she seems very level headed, from what I've seen."

"Well, I think she'd love it, and I don't have a problem. I could ask her." Tessa filled up their water glasses. "Would it be on weekends?"

"Ideally. We'd be looking at several locations. A sports stadium, beach volleyball, waterslides, that type of thing.

Depending on the locations, it will most likely be spread out over a couple of months, a day or two, here and there. There's likely to be a bit of ongoing work from it too. It could be a bit of extra income for her, but it wouldn't interfere too much with her sports, or her school work."

Chris came back with a table number and sat down. "Have you asked her?"

"I just did." Flea reached into her handbag and pulled out a business card. "Here, give Abigail my number and we'll get together to talk about it. It'll pay well and she can bring school work along on the shoots, if she needs to."

Tessa took the card and tucked it into her pocket.

"I'm starving." Flea pulled her sunglasses back down and stretched her long legs out in the sun. She was wearing jogging shorts and sneakers. "I'm going to need sustenance if I'm going to run home again later."

They sat in the morning sun and chatted. Tessa quickly posted on her Instagram page some of the photos Chris had sent her. The coffee arrived, followed soon after by their meals. Her fruit with coconut yoghurt was lovely and very colourful, but watching Flea enthusiastically digging into hash browns, eggs and sautéed mushrooms gave her serious food envy.

"So, I guess we're related now," Flea said, sipping her smoothie. "How weird is that?" Tessa squirmed in her seat, feeling awkward and unable to look at Chris. "Do I call you Aunty Tessa?" Flea asked.

Karithopita
(spiced walnut cake)

Ingredients:

125 g butter, softened

170 g caster sugar

4 eggs, separated

80 ml brandy

1 Tbsp finely grated orange rind

1 tsp ground cinnamon

1/2 tsp ground cloves

230 g finely chopped walnuts

150 g self-raising flour

100 g walnuts, coarsely chopped, plus extra to garnish

1 tsp ground cinnamon, plus extra to garnish

Spiced syrup:

125 ml water

80 ml orange juice

200 g caster sugar

4 whole cloves

1 cinnamon stick

Method:

Preheat the oven to 180°C. Grease and line the base of a 20 cm square cake pan with baking paper.

Use an electric mixer to beat the butter and sugar together until pale and creamy. Add the egg yolks, one at a time, beating well between each addition. Add the brandy, rind, cinnamon and cloves and stir to combine. Add the finely chopped walnuts and flour and stir to combine.

Place egg whites in a clean, dry bowl. Use an electric mixer to whisk until firm peaks form. Add one-third of the egg white to the walnut mixture and fold until just combined. Add remaining egg white and fold to combine. Pour mixture into pan and smooth the surface.

Bake for 40 minutes or until a skewer inserted in the centre comes out clean when tested. Remove from the oven.

To make the syrup, combine all ingredients in a saucepan over low heat. Cook, stirring, for 2–3 minutes or until sugar dissolves. Increase heat to medium-high and bring to a simmer. Cook for 3–4 minutes or until syrup thickens slightly. Remove from heat and discard cloves and cinnamon stick.

Turn cake onto a wire rack over an oven tray. Pour the hot syrup evenly over the cake. Combine the extra walnuts and extra cinnamon in a bowl. Sprinkle evenly over the cake. Pour any syrup that collects on the oven tray over the cake for a second time. Serve warm or at room temperature.

Eleni

"Who is this woman anyway? This stranger you want to bring into my house?" Savvas refused to turn off the television despite the fact that the caregiver was coming to meet them.

"Her name is Barbara, and I told you already: Alan, the nurse at Mamá's rest home, recommended her." Eleni put the still-warm cake under the dome and flicked the jug on.

"Alan. Bah. What kind of man is a nurse anyway? A fag, that's who." The doorbell rang.

"Savvas, don't use that word!" Eleni said, hoping the caregiver hadn't heard him.

She went to the door, her hands clammy. A woman stood on the other side. It was hard to tell how old she was — she could have been anywhere from fifty to eighty. Built like a tank, she was almost as wide as she was tall. Her hair was cut short around her weathered face and she wore a long-sleeved T-shirt with a *T rex* dinosaur on the front, a speech bubble coming from its mouth that said 'I hate push-ups'.

"You must be Eleni," she said, smiling widely. She had a gold canine tooth.

"Please, come in." Eleni stepped back to show her down the hallway and into the lounge. "Can I offer you tea? Coffee? I made karithopita. It's a walnut cake."

"Sounds wonderful, darlin'." Barbara gave Eleni's lower bicep a comforting squeeze. She had very warm hands. "But let's meet your gorgeous young man first, shall we?"

Theo was in the lounge with Savvas, lining up his sea turtles across the coffee table in some sort of order. Barbara took in the scene and then went over to Theo, where she squatted down.

"Hello there, handsome," she said. "I'm Barbara, your new friend."

"Say hello to Barbara, Theo," Eleni prompted. He ignored her. "And this is Savvas, my husband," she added. Savvas gave Barbara a curt nod and went back to watching the sports channel.

"Theo," Barbara said. "Did you know that there's an aquarium near here with turtles?" Theo looked up.

"I see the turtles?" he asked Eleni.

"I might take you to see the turtles if you're a good guy for me when I come to visit," Barbara said. Theo finally looked at her briefly, then looked away.

"Hello, Barbara," he said. "You want to see a magic trick?"

"I do, Theo," Barbara said. "How about you show Mum and me your trick while Dad puts the kettle on?" She moved over to stand in front of the TV screen, blocking a large portion of it. Savvas scowled at her. She looked unfazed. "Tea with milk and two, thanks, buddy," she said, giving Eleni a little wink.

Eleni watched Savvas out of the corner of her eye as he went into the kitchen. He took down mugs and then banged about the kitchen, looking for tea bags, opening cupboards and then finally finding them in the caddy next to the electric jug. Barbara hadn't missed a thing and had a thoughtful look on her face.

"Here's my magic turtles." Theo covered two of the turtles with plastic cups. "Guess which one where the turtle is."

Barbara pointed to the red cup. "I'm going to guess that one."

"No. Wrong." He lifted both cups off. "It's all of them." He howled with laughter, rolling onto his side on the carpet.

"Great trick, Theo. I like it. How about you go and get some water in one of those cups to have with our cake and we'll sit up at the table."

Eleni headed towards the kitchen to help Savvas with the cake but Barbara laid a gentle hand on her arm. "If you don't mind, Eleni, you and I can start going over the questionnaire. I can see your husband has got things under control. A large piece of cake for me, please, Savvas. I skipped lunch today."

• • •

The questions Barbara asked were easy enough to answer. They were mostly about Theo's history and his current routine, likes and dislikes. Savvas even sat with them for the first half hour before he mumbled something about the garden and disappeared outside into the shed.

"I'm so sorry about my husband," Eleni said, leaning forward and almost whispering to Barbara.

"Don't you worry about him. He's not the first dad I've come across who doesn't think it's his responsibility to pull his weight. It will be an adjustment for him but, believe me, there will be changes around here. I take it he doesn't have much input into Theo's day-to-day care?"

"No. Well, he does babysit him when I need to go out. He works part time at a packaging company and I work as a caregiver, but my boss is away on his honeymoon at the moment."

Barbara had put a pair of reading glasses on and now peered sternly at Eleni over their rims. "He's not babysitting, he's parenting. Don't you forget that."

Eleni didn't mention the incident where Theo had gone missing, as she'd told Barbara in the initial email that that had been the catalyst for finding more care for Theo. It was definitely on her mind though.

"Theo is at a care centre four days a week, but I'm finding it hard to manage him in the evenings. I also think he needs more outings in the community. To be honest, it's not easy taking him out. It's quite exhausting."

"I agree with you. How about we come up with a bit of a schedule? I can come in on Theo's day off and also a couple of evenings to start with. I'm happy to run a hoover around and fold washing as well, that kind of thing."

Savvas had slunk back into the room, lurking near the TV

but not turning it on. He scowled as though he had expected Barbara to be gone by then.

"Does Theo do his own care? Showering and such?"

Eleni sighed. "No, he refuses to wash himself, or his hair. I tend to do it, but only every second day. Again, it's a bit of a trial."

"Well, we can't have that." She beckoned Savvas over. "No man wants his mother to see his privates in the shower, do they? Not at his age. From now on, Savvas, you will shower Theo. Every second night will be fine. You will also supervise and tidy up after his breakfast every morning. That will be a start."

Savvas opened his mouth to say something, then shut it and nodded meekly.

Barbara briskly packed her notes into a folder with Scooby-Doo prints on the front. "Now, if you're wanting to go ahead, how about I start next week?"

• • •

When Barbara left, Eleni expected Savvas to go off at her. To start yelling that he wouldn't have her in the house and that they couldn't afford it.

"Barbara is my friend," Theo said. "We're going to see the turtles."

Savvas looked at Theo, muttered something incoherent and then disappeared back outside to his garden shed.

It was blissfully quiet with the TV off.

Abigail

Sometimes Maddy can be a bit of a cow. When she said she liked Levi, I didn't think much about it. She likes heaps of guys. Anyone who's hot, really. She thinks Mr Bacon is kind of hot too, but it's not like she's going to hook up with him, is it?

But just because Levi likes me and not her, she's being all bitchy.

"I'm just saying, it's sisters before misters," she says. Again.

"What about that time in year ten when I told you I thought Jayden was cute and then you made out with him at Cooper's party?"

"It was spin the bottle," she says. It was, but I'm pretty sure the bottle was closer to Simon Eggert than Jayden. And then she told me they were going out all that week and that he was into her and didn't know who I was. I don't say anything about that, even though he told me last year that on his spin he'd been hoping the bottle would land on me that night.

"Anyway, it's so weird going out with your neighbour," she says. "Like, what about when you break up? And then you have to see him all the time."

I want to say that we might not break up but I know she'll say that I'm naive.

"But it's handy for hanging out," I say, trying to keep it light, "and I never saw him all the time before anyway."

"I bet he's been watching you get changed for years," she laughs. "Levi the perv."

"Don't say shit like that," I tell her. I'm actually pissed off now. I kind of wonder why I'm even friends with her, to be honest.

"Well, anyway, it doesn't even matter. I like Todd way better than Levi. He's got a better body, and Levi has a big nose."

God, I hate her sometimes.

"Well, you know what they say about big noses," I say, with a laugh, even though I've hardly done anything with Levi yet, let alone seen how big his dick is. It was too dark to see anything the other night when he dropped the flag.

"Whatever," she says. "He seems like he's a bit desperate for a girlfriend, if you ask me."

I hang up on her.

Everything Sauce

Ingredients:

1 avocado

1 cup packed parsley and coriander leaves (or basil if you hate coriander)

1 jalapeño pepper, ribs and seeds removed

2 cloves garlic

juice of 1 or 2 limes

1/2 cup water

1/2 cup olive oil

1 tsp salt

1/2 cup pistachios or other nuts (use sunflower seeds to replace nuts if you have an allergy)

Method:

Blend everything except the nuts to a puree. Add the nuts last and blend to the desired consistency.

This can be served as a dip, spread or sauce — or add additional water or oil to thin the sauce for use as a dressing or a marinade. It's compatible with everything: salads, chicken, chips and crackers, sandwiches, dipping vegetables, you name it.

Tessa

Brady arrived that night as Tessa was putting her 'Everything Sauce' on the salad and thinking about what to use it for when Chris came to do the next shoot. Thomas had grilled the chicken for her, while Abigail sat texting furiously on her phone the whole time before being made to set the table.

"Sorry I'm late, I had to drop Jess off to work 'cause her battery died and the traffic was shite."

"Where does she work? I forgot." Tessa gave him a nod when he waved a bottle of Pinot at her in question.

"She does retail at the airport in one of the duty-free stores. Gets a great discount on alcohol."

"Is she old enough to drink it though?" Tessa grinned as her brother threw her a dirty look.

"She's not that young," he said, pouring the wines. Then he got a sly look on his face that Tessa didn't like. "Anyway, have you never shagged anyone younger than yourself?"

Tessa pretended to scratch her nose with her middle finger up. "So, Abigail is going out with Levi," she said to change the subject. "After he declared his love, naked, wrapped in a Samoan flag on the back lawn." Brady and Thomas both cracked up and Abigail pretended to be offended, but was beaming.

"How's the flatting going?" Brady asked Thomas.

"Pretty good. It's a bit of a pain sorting out meals and cleaning and stuff, but it's okay."

"How many of you are there? This is good chicken, by the way."

"Yeah, it's Mum's marinade. There's me and Aidan from work and a chick called Joan and her partner, Taylor. I haven't met Taylor yet though. They're away heaps for their job."

"He hasn't even come home with laundry yet," Tessa said. "So he's doing better than you, Brady."

"But I have an alcohol source now, so you'll want to keep being nice to me."

"Can I put in an order for a nice gin then? Maybe that black one?"

"I'll see what I can do."

"Levi says his mum is making him go to his tinamatua tomorrow after school as punishment for the flag," Abigail said, reading off her phone. "His dad's mum. He has to cut her toenails."

"Gross, not at the table," Thomas complained. He had a

thing about feet, but not like foot-fetish Gary — more of a can't stand them thing.

"This sauce is so good," Brady said as they ate. "You should think about selling it."

"Ha ha, you're so funny." Tessa rolled her eyes.

"How's business going anyway?"

"Really good. Sales are up since I started getting my act together with my website and on social media. I'm on Instagram now, you know."

Abigail gave her one of her teenaged 'looks'. Like it was unbearable to be related.

"I hope it's not lame," she said, in the voice of someone who clearly expected it to be lame.

"What's your Insta handle?" Thomas asked, picking up his phone.

"SaucyTessa," she said, and Abigail groaned.

"Gross, Mum."

They both did that speedy thing with their fingers that no one over thirty can achieve and found her page within seconds. Then Abigail let out a piercing shriek.

"Oh. My. God. Kill me now!"

"Umm, Mum," Thomas said, looking at her and back at the phone. "Did you post that on purpose?"

"What?" Tessa picked up her own phone and punched in the lock screen code. So did Brady.

"Whoa, sis. That's a pretty raunchy shot," he said, raising

his eyebrows.

"This is mortifying," Abigail said. "I can never show my face at school again."

"What on earth are you all going on about?" Tessa said, finally getting into her page.

She thought she might be sick. Bile rose in the back of her throat as she looked at the picture sitting on her page for everyone to see. It was supposed to be a bowl of pesto spaghetti, adorned with basil and sprinkled with Parmesan shavings. Instead, she'd posted the picture of herself half naked in her dressing gown. She felt like she might faint.

"It's got a heap of likes," Thomas said helpfully.

"It was supposed to be spaghetti," Tessa said. 'Oh my God, what the hell? It's supposed to be pesto."

Brady was trying not to laugh. Abigail was still shrieking about how embarrassed she was. Tessa felt like the room had erupted in flames. She was living a nightmare.

"How do I get rid of it?" she yelled, pushing at buttons. "Bloody hell, I can't remember how to delete things. Abigail, shut up and help me."

Thomas took her phone from her and pushed a few buttons.

"There, it's gone," he said.

Tessa sat with her head in her hands. She was beyond mortified. Brady topped up her wine.

"Still, it was a nice picture of you, Mum," Thomas said, patting her back awkwardly. "Who took it anyway?"

She was truly in the depths of hell. She looked desperately at Brady for help, but he wasn't picking up her distress signal.

"Um, I … Um …" She picked up her glass and took a large glug.

"Oh my God," Abigail said. "It was Mr Bacon, wasn't it?"

• • •

She had to come clean. She was a terrible liar and nothing else made sense to explain why she had that photo. She couldn't have taken it herself, and it was obviously not an old picture.

"So you're seeing Mr Bacon?" Thomas said, getting himself another beer. Tessa nodded. "How old is he then?"

"He's *so* much younger than Mum," Abigail said. "He's probably only like forty."

"He's thirty-nine, actually," Tessa mumbled. "And I'm only forty-six, thank you."

"He looks older though, don't you think?" Brady directed this at the table. "It's probably the lack of hair, I reckon, it makes him look older. He kind of looks like Jason Statham, actually."

"Thank God I'm not talking to Maddy at the moment," Abigail said. "She would literally die."

"Why aren't you talking to Maddy?" Tessa asked.

"I don't want to talk about it," Abigail said. "And stop trying to change the subject. This is a nightmare for me. I'm going to have to change schools or, like, go to boarding school where nobody knows me."

"Have you told Mum you're seeing each other?" Brady asked.

"No, and don't you tell her either. I'll tell her when they get back."

"Eww, it's like incest," Abigail declared, making a gagging noise.

"It is not," Thomas said. "Stop being such a drama queen." He gave his sister a whack on her shoulder with the back of his hand. "Anyway, it's cool. He seems like a good dude, Mum, so if you're happy, we're happy. Right, Abs?"

"No," Abigail said. "I am not happy."

Afghan Biscuits

Ingredients:

250 g butter, softened

3/4 cup brown sugar

1/4 cup cocoa

1 2/3 cups plain flour

2 1/2 cups cornflakes

Chocolate icing:

1 1/2 cups icing sugar mixture

2 Tbsp cocoa powder

2 Tbsp hot water

walnuts, to decorate

Method:

Preheat the oven to 180℃/160℃ fan-forced. Grease 2 large baking trays and line with baking paper.

Using an electric mixer, beat butter and sugar together until light and fluffy. Add cocoa and flour. Beat on low speed until combined. Stir in cornflakes.

Roll level tablespoons of mixture into balls. Flatten slightly. Place onto prepared trays, 4 cm apart, to allow room for spreading during cooking.

Bake for 15—18 minutes or until just firm to the touch, swapping trays halfway through cooking. Cool completely on trays.

To make chocolate icing, sift the icing sugar and cocoa into a bowl. Gradually stir in enough hot water until the mixture is smooth and combined.

Spoon icing onto the tops of the biscuits, spreading slightly. Decorate with walnuts. Set aside for 1 hour to set. Serve.

Tessa

Sonya was hanging a picture when Tessa knocked on the ranch slider and then slid it open. She looked over from the dining room chair she was standing on.

"Does that look straight to you?"

Tessa tilted her head to the side. "Left side down a bit," she said.

Sonya adjusted the picture and climbed down. "There. What do you think?"

'Perfect. It's gorgeous."

"Levi took it last year for his art portfolio and I've been meaning to get it framed and hung. He was photographing down near the old railway line."

"It's beautiful. He has an eye." Levi had captured a sunset, the sky in hues of pinks and purples with the old wooden bridge in the background. "He has Chris, doesn't he?"

"As a teacher? Yeah. Cuppa?"

"Yes, thanks."

Sonya took two mugs from the cupboard. "So, how's that going anyway?"

Tessa tried and failed not to smile. "Um, to be honest ... pretty great."

"Green tea with jasmine or regular?"

"Green ... no, regular."

Sonya made the tea and they took it to the living room, where they curled up on the worn but comfy blue velvet sofas Sonya and Alofa had had forever.

"Do the kids know?"

"Yes. I don't think Abs is happy about it, but she's a teenager, so there's plenty she's not happy about at the moment." Tessa took one of Sonya's Afghan biscuits off the plate and bit into it.

Sonya gave her a look. "I didn't want to say anything, but I'm glad to see you enjoying food again. I think your negative body image has been affecting Abigail. Whenever she's here, she barely eats a thing."

"Really? I thought it was a training thing. She's been going on about eating less carbs lately."

"She needs the carbs if she's training though, doesn't she? I wish women would realise that being healthy and confident and loving yourself is attractive, and that doesn't mean everyone has to be stick thin. Honestly, society can take a flying leap for all the body image damage it's done."

"Maybe you could try giving her a pep talk like you did to me. Sorry it took me so long to listen." Tessa took another bite. "By the way, these biscuits are bloody delicious."

She had a date that night with Chris and she had something to celebrate. CoHab Wholefoods had agreed to stock part of her range in their stores and, although they were only taking a few products for now, it was a great start. This would be a huge boost in sales for Tessa. If everything went to plan, they'd increase the range later in the year. The National Sales Manager had been hugely enthusiastic, and Tessa was feeling positive.

• • •

At the restaurant, Martinas, they were offered a table in the window, but Chris asked for a booth, which was way more secluded and romantic. He ordered bubbly and proposed a toast, reaching out and holding her hand across the table.

"I'm incredibly proud of you and everything you've achieved."

"It's partly thanks to your photos too," she said, trying not to think of the photo she'd accidentally posted on Instagram, and how many people it had reached before Thomas had deleted it for her.

"To hard work, and sexy photos." He clinked glasses and winked. It was like he could read her mind.

Chris ordered papoutsakia and groaned appreciatively at every bite. He was a man who loved his food, Tessa thought.

"Man, this tastes just like the one Eleni makes us sometimes," he said. "Her mum, Cora, used to make it when we were little kids when we went to Grandad's for dinner. Greek food is my comfort food, I think."

"What about your mum?" Tessa asked. "Does she cook much?"

"The only thing Margot makes well is a dry martini," Chris told her. "All us kids love food, but we'd have never made it through childhood without food deliveries and Cora's cooking."

"So Cora was Howard's housekeeper? And then Eleni? I remember her from the wedding."

"Yeah. After Cora got Alzheimer's, Eleni took over her job. She used to be a nurse, but she got sick of it, I think. And she's got a special needs kid, so the flexible hours worked for her." He scraped the last of the stuffed eggplant from his plate and sat back contentedly. "Do you think your mum will want to keep Eleni on after they get back?"

"Oh, I'd think so. I can't imagine Mum wanting to clean if she doesn't have to. And she's no good with medical stuff. She barely used to keep a packet of plasters in the house when we were kids, and I don't think we even owned a thermometer." Tessa finished her main and took a sip of wine. "It's weird, I hadn't even thought about the fact that she'll be moving when she gets back. She'll be so much further away."

"She seems like a good lady, your mum," Chris said. "She's looking good for her age too. Good genes. We Bacon men have great taste."

Afterwards they went dancing. Tessa hadn't been to a club for years; she loved to dance, but Keith hadn't. Surprisingly, they weren't the oldest people there. Chris said he 'had it on good authority' — from the students he taught — that this wasn't a cool place for the kids, and when the music switched to something slow he pulled her in close and wrapped his arms around her waist. Tessa closed her eyes and listened to the music and to Chris humming softly, although a bit tunelessly, in her ear. It was lovely, but he was pressed up against her and all she could think about was getting back home and pressing closer.

"Shall we go?" she whispered.

...

The streets were still bustling with people as they got into her car, Chris driving because Tessa had had too much champagne. Unable to wait, she leant across their seats before they'd even had time to fasten their seatbelts and kissed him fiercely, hoping it might give him an incentive to get home faster. The car was small and there wasn't much room. Tessa's elbow hit the horn, and the loud sharp blast had passers-by gaping at the couple who were, probably, way too old to be making out in public.

There was a rap at the passenger window. Tessa leapt back in her seat in horror. Flea was grinning at them, indicating for Tessa to wind the window down. She did, reluctantly.

"Ha, caught out," Flea cackled.

"We ... we're celebrating my business. Chris's photos have made such a difference ..."

"If this is how he charges his clients, remind me never to use my brother for a photo shoot then." Both she and Chris made identical disgusted faces at the thought.

"Carry on, none of my business what you get up to in private. Although, this is, perhaps, a little bit public." She laughed again, gave them a wave and Tessa wound up the window. Chris cleared his throat. "Well, that was a bit awkward," he said. "I guess now I won't be able to hold it over her the time I caught her smoking weed out her bedroom window."

"Cat's out of the bag," Tessa said.

Chris reached over and fastened her seat belt, then his own.

"I hope she doesn't feel she has to share with everyone," he said. He smiled at her. "Let's get home. I've got better things to think about than my sister."

Lemon Risotto

....

Ingredients:

6 cups chicken stock

3 1/2 Tbsp butter

1 1/2 Tbsp olive oil

2 large shallots, chopped

2 cups Arborio rice or medium-grain white rice

1/4 cup dry white wine

1 cup/85 g freshly grated Parmesan cheese

2 Tbsp chopped fresh parsley

2 Tbsp fresh lemon juice

4 tsp grated lemon peel

Method:

Bring stock to a simmer in a large saucepan over medium heat. Reduce the heat to low and cover to keep warm. Melt 1 1/2 tablespoons butter with oil in a heavy large saucepan over medium heat. Add shallots and sauté until tender, about 6 minutes. Add rice and stir for 1 minute. Add wine and stir until evaporated, about 30 seconds. Add 1 1/2 cups hot stock and simmer until absorbed, stirring frequently. Add remaining stock 1/2 cup at a time, allowing stock to be absorbed before adding more, and stirring frequently until rice is creamy and tender, about 35 minutes. Stir in cheese and remaining 2 tablespoons butter. Stir in parsley, lemon juice and lemon peel. Season risotto with salt and pepper. Transfer to bowl and serve.

Tessa

Despite her mortification, the Instagram faux pas had done wonders for her business. Sales had increased and Tessa found herself struggling to keep up. The local paper contacted her to do a small piece and she was described as 'Nigella Saucon', which made Chris laugh. She found herself having to work late at night to make large sauce batches, label bottles and send out orders, never mind keeping up with the bookwork. It was getting harder and harder to fit everything in.

"I hate to say it, Tessa, but I think you might have to give all this glamour and glory up," Prisha told her one day as they made up cellophane gift packs for Easter. "It may be time to leave the Forest nest and fly free."

"I know." Tessa finished tying a ribbon and looked at her colleague. "But I'm scared. What if I fail? And I'll miss you so much."

"You won't fail, and I'll be here. We can get lunch, if you're not rushed off your feet."

"I'll always make time for you, Prish. If I'm that rushed off my feet, I'll have to get you to stick labels on bottles while we eat."

"Deal. So, you think you'll do it?"

Tessa sighed. "I think I'll have to. I'm so tired, I put my car keys in the fridge and the butter in my handbag yesterday."

"Messy."

"Yep, and trying to get it clean was just another thing to have to do."

Prisha put away the scissors she'd been using to cut lengths of blue and silver ribbon. "You can always come back." Her forehead wrinkled as she thought. "How about this: I'll get that lazy-arse daughter of mine to come in and help on the weekend. She could do with the pocket money and she's been talking for ages about finding a job. Over the winter when it's quiet, I'm sure I can manage on my own during the week. Once it gets busy again, you can decide whether you want to come back. If not, I'll find someone permanent."

"You'd do that?"

"Of course. I may as well start writing an advert now though, because you won't look back, Tess. You're going to fly, I know it."

. . .

Tessa arrived home, brought in the mail and went straight to the kitchen to wipe down the bottles of kasundi she'd made the night before to get them ready for labelling. She threw the mail onto the bench, and noticed one of the envelopes was made of thick cream paper, her name and address written in neat calligraphy. Inside was an invitation and a typed letter.

It is with great pleasure we inform you that you have been nominated for the Artisan Foods 'Newcomer to the Industry' award. We would like to cordially invite you to the awards ceremony to take place Saturday the 22nd of April at the Royal Towers Hotel.

Please RSVP with guest numbers before Saturday the 15th of April.

We look forward to seeing you there.

Kind regards

Christine Zhou

Artisan Foods Committee Secretary

Tessa was thrilled. She picked up her phone and found Chris's number, then paused. He was the first person she had wanted to tell, she realised. In a short space of time he had become someone so important to her. It was a little bit scary. Especially because she didn't know how he really felt about her, or where their relationship was going. Was it too soon to be feeling like this might be serious? All she knew was she wanted him to be there with her in these moments. She wanted him with her to celebrate. She rang his phone.

After she finished her labels, she made salmon steaks and lemon risotto for dinner and chilled a bottle of Chablis. Chris arrived with a wrapped box and gave her a long kiss.

"Congratulations, gorgeous." He handed over his gift. It was very heavy and Tessa set it on the bench before she lifted the lid. "It took me four shops to find one that was right."

Inside was a garden gnome. It was holding a gold trophy in one hand, its white beard and hat covered in streamers. "Do you like it?" He looked so earnest that Tessa felt terrible. She gave Chris a hug.

"I do. But I have to tell you something." She pulled back, looking up at his face. "I hate garden gnomes."

"What? What do you mean? You collect them."

"I do. But as a joke. Let's have a drink, shall we." She pulled out glasses and opened the wine while she explained. "After Keith left me, we had to sort out a lot of stuff, including who got the house. I wanted to keep it, mainly for the kids, so things didn't change too much for them. Keith agreed, but on the condition that he use the garden to advertise his landscaping business." She poured them both a glass of wine. "He maintains the gardens and stuff as part of the deal. But it started to piss me off how he was waltzing in and out and treating the place like he still lived here. I mentioned it to Sonya and then one day she turned up with a garden gnome. She did it because she knew how much Keith would hate it. It kind of became a long-standing joke. She buys me one every year for Christmas and my birthday."

She looked up at Chris for his reaction, passing him a glass. He laughed loudly, then raised his glass in toast.

"To you, Tessa. Goddess in the kitchen and mastermind of revenge." They tapped glasses, grinning at each other.

"It was Sonya's devious plan, to be fair," she said, "but thank you for my gift."

...

Abigail arrived home as they were loading the dishwasher. She scowled when she saw Chris and then complained that she was starving and that she would never get her licence if no one ever let her drive anywhere. She was in a particularly foul mood.

"I'll try to take you in the weekend," Tessa said. "Maybe if you helped me with some of my labelling, we could go out on Sunday?"

"You get all nervous and freak out though. It makes me nervous. I miss Gran."

"You know, I failed my licence twice," Chris told her.

"Is that why you bike to school?" Abigail asked, making him laugh.

"No, I can drive. I like biking. It keeps me fit and it's better for the environment too. My point is that I ended up getting professional lessons. My parents were hopeless teachers and my grandfather was passing on some terrible habits to me. I think he might have been given his licence without sitting the test, to be honest. He's from a very small farming town. No traffic lights. One roundabout." He took a cloth and wiped down the table. "The instructor was good. He pointed out all my errors and took me around the test course and I passed it the third time with no drama."

"Can I get lessons?" Abigail looked at her mum.

"Absolutely." It was nice not having to worry about the cost for once.

"What's your mobile number, Abigail?" Chris opened his phone and fiddled around and then Abigail's phone dinged.

"That's the number of a mate of mine who does lessons. They're usually pretty busy, but tell him I sent you. He owes me a favour."

"Okay. Thanks." Tessa wasn't sure if that was directed at her or Chris.

"I'm up for an award for my business," she told Abigail.

"Cool," Abigail said absently, climbing the stairs, already on her phone.

Chris's
Blueberry Pancakes

....

Ingredients:

3/4 cup milk

2 Tbsp white vinegar

1 cup flour

2 Tbsp sugar

1 tsp baking powder

1/2 tsp baking soda

1/2 tsp salt

1 egg

2 Tbsp melted butter, plus more for the pan

1 cup or more fresh blueberries

Method:

Mix the milk and vinegar and let it sit for a minute or two (you're making 'buttermilk').

Whisk the dry ingredients together. Whisk the egg, buttermilk and melted butter into the dry ingredients until just combined.

Heat a nonstick pan over medium heat. Melt a little smear of butter in the pan (for a golden-brown crust).

Pour about 1/3 cup of batter into the hot pan and spread it flat (it will be pretty thick). Arrange a few blueberries on top. Cook until you see little bubbles on top and the edges starting to firm up. Flip and cook for another 1–2 minutes until the pancakes are sky-high fluffy and cooked through.

Serve with maple syrup and bacon.

Tessa

Chris had slept over. It was the first time he'd done it and Tessa had been a little nervous about Abigail's reaction, but she had been up and gone to an early game before Tessa was even fully awake.

"I'm going to make you breakfast," Chris told her with a kiss, getting out of bed and putting on her dressing gown. It looked both ridiculous and weirdly sexy on him. It was far too short for one thing, and very feminine, but somehow he pulled it off with style. "I'll make you my famous blueberry pancakes," he called over his shoulder as he disappeared down the stairs.

She must have dozed off for a while but the sound of a lawnmower woke her back up.

She threw on some clothes and brushed her teeth, making her way downstairs where she could smell breakfast cooking. Chris had set the table for two, with a sprig of lavender in one of her jars as the centrepiece. When he saw her, he motioned her to sit and flipped a pancake before opening the oven door and pulling out a plate of crispy bacon and a stack of pancakes. "Coffee or tea? I normally do tea in the mornings."

She realised they were starting to get to know each other's habits now. "Tea for me too," she said. "Just milk."

He plated the last pancake and slid the hot pan into the sink before joining her and tucking in.

"These are good." Tessa cut off another bite of pancake.

"Thanks, it's the vinegar in the milk that does it. I'm glad you like them, 'cause apart from these and spaghetti bolognese, I'm pretty hopeless in the kitchen, to be honest."

There was a bang on the sliding door and Tessa looked up in surprise. Keith was standing there in a pair of gumboots, a scowl on his face.

Tessa got up and opened the door a little bit. "Yes?"

"I've put up a new sign. Should be more visible. Can you make sure nobody parks right outside?" Keith glanced over at Chris, who was still tucking into his breakfast as though he hadn't noticed the interruption.

"Well, Keith, I can't control where people park, but I personally won't park in front of the sign."

"So, who's that then?" He tilted his head in a weird way, as though he had a crick in his neck, towards Chris.

"Keith, this is Chris. Chris, the father of my children, Keith."

"Hey, man." Chris waved his fork at Keith and went back

to cutting his pancake.

Keith did a weird nod.

"Anyway, I need to trim the privet. I'll have to get back to do it later. I've got to take Kael to the park while Racquel has a class."

"I could do that for you," Chris said. "Save you coming back later."

Keith snorted. "I don't need you messing with things in my garden, *mate*." The 'mate' was stated very clearly. In a very un-matey way. "Leave it to the professionals, all right?"

"Whatever you say. Wouldn't want to cock it up."

"Could you maybe do it next week? It's a bit noisy for a Saturday," Tessa asked.

"Tessa, I don't run to your schedule. As it is, I'll have to do it tomorrow. I haven't got time today since I have to get back to pick up Abigail in a bit. Racquel hates when I work Sunday too. I'll have to miss family meditation." Chris did a funny little half cough, half laugh, and Tessa tried not to snicker. "Abigail needs to sit her licence. All this running around after her is a pain in the arse," Keith said, looking, Tessa had to say, like the whole meditation thing wasn't doing much for him yet.

"Well, maybe you could let her drive today? She needs all the practice she can get."

"My truck's less than a year old, Tessa," he snorted, as if that was an explanation, before he turned and went back down the stairs. "And tell loverboy to keep away from my hedge. I don't need some dick making a mess of it."

"It's actually *my* hedge," Tessa called to his retreating back.

• • •

Tessa procrastinated starting on her work after Chris left by doing an inventory of her spice drawer and sorting her cupboard of plastic containers. Abigail came home happy. They had won their game and she'd been awarded player of the day. She helped herself to the leftover pancakes and Tessa forced herself not to query what had happened to the no-carbs diet.

"Flea rang me," she said around a mouthful. "We need to be at the sports stadium at six next Saturday for the first photo shoot. She said to ask you if you wanted to be in the stands as an extra, since you have to be there as my legal guardian."

"Sure. May as well," Tessa agreed.

"These are good pancakes, they taste different than normal." Abigail finished off the last one and pulled her hair out of her scrunchie. "Eugh, I still smell like chlorine. And I need some more of that blue shampoo."

"I'll get some this afternoon. Chris made the pancakes actually," Tessa said as she tidied up. Abigail scowled. She looked like her father when she did that, the little furrow between her eyebrows matching Keith's.

"Seriously, Mum, it's so gross you dating Mr Bacon. He's

young and good looking and you're like ..."

"I'm what, Abigail?"

"You know ... You."

Tessa wasn't sure if that had made her more angry or hurt, but either way, she was a bit over the teenaged attitude. She wondered if she had been this self-centred with her mother. She probably had. She could only hope that she and Abigail came through it all and ended up friends like she and Vanda were. She missed her mum. This was the longest she had gone without talking to her in years.

"Well, there's no accounting for taste, I guess," she said quietly. "Now if you could move all your gear, I need to get some work done in here if you want me to be done in time to take you to your first driving lesson."

...

Once Abigail left the kitchen, Tessa got busy making a batch of chocolate sauce. Sonya had dropped off a massive load of feijoas from their hedge and she needed to get them peeled too for her chutney. She was also running low on lemon curd. It was good that business was so good, but she was starting to feel the pressure. She needed to concentrate full time on it, and the part-time job was going to have to go. She did some calculations in her head as she cooked, working out her finances. She was optimistic that things would go well.

The kitchen smelt like chocolate, warm and rich with a hint of vanilla. It reminded her of Chris and the first photo shoot and she smiled. Abigail would be horrified if she found out what they had done on this very kitchen counter, she thought, with a little laugh.

• • •

While Abigail had her driving lesson, Tessa did a grocery shop and picked up Abigail's special swimmer's shampoo. She contemplated looking for a dress for the awards ceremony and then decided she would wear the dress she had worn to the wedding. It wasn't as if she was likely to win, she reasoned, and although the business was doing well, she found it hard to justify the money for an expensive dress she would probably wear only once. Besides, she thought, Chris had liked her in that dress.

They were planning to stay overnight in the city after the awards. Chris said his family owned an apartment overlooking the water and that they could use it. She was looking forward to a little mini break with him, and a fancy night out.

• • •

After dropping Abigail at Maddy's, Tessa pulled up outside the house, parking well away from Keith's sign. Chris was there, coming from the back lawn. He had a smudge of dirt on his forehead and a twig clung to his sleeve. He gave her a weird, almost sheepish look. She got out of the car, opened her mouth to say something and stopped.

There was a large Irish yew tree in the front yard, next

to Keith's newly erected sign. Now the tree was also newly erected. Chris had trimmed it. It was sculpted into an impressively realistic phallic shape, with a mushroom head and two round balls at its base. It looked exactly like a massive penis.

"Before you say anything," Chris said, sounding a bit nervous, "I googled and found which trees could be used for topiary. And it will be easy enough to trim it back. Shit, I hope you're not mad? I didn't touch the hedge, but I guess your ex annoyed me a little bit this morning and ..." he trailed off. "I can't tell what you're thinking."

Tessa burst out laughing. She roared with laughter. She laughed until tears leaked out and she couldn't catch her breath, hunched over on the front path, laughing like a loon. It was brilliant.

"God, I love you," she said with a grin.

Abigail

I'm on the phone to Maddy.

"I can't believe your mum is dating Mr Bacon," she says
for the thousandth time. "How cringe for you."

"He's actually not bad," I tell her. "He's quite funny and
it's not like I take any of his subjects."

"Well, I'd be so embarrassed if it was me."

I am totally embarrassed. Like, I could die, embarrassed.
But I don't comment, so when the silence goes on too long
she changes the subject.

"Deanna is having a party in a couple of weeks. Like, on
the long weekend." I can hear her inhaling.

"Are you smoking?" I ask.

"Gross, no one our age smokes, Abs. It's a vape. It's watermelon flavoured."

"They're literally as bad. Anyway, I'm doing the modelling
job that weekend, remember?"

Maddy does a weird little laugh. "It's so funny how you say

that, like it's a proper job or something, instead of a thing because Felicia Bacon's brother is banging your mum."

Man, she can be such a bitch. We've only just made up after the fight when Levi asked me out and she was all pissy at me because she said I knew she liked him first. It's not my fault he likes me and not her. And you can't call dibs on a person. Now she's being a cow about me modelling. Levi reckons she's jealous. And he thinks she's super vain and that I'm way nicer.

"I'm getting paid, and it's a whole ad campaign, not just one shoot. She picked me for it because I have the right look, not because she knows me."

"Is it plus size then?" she asks and then laughs. "Just kidding," she adds, but I know she isn't.

"Anyway, back to this weekend. Why wouldn't you have a party? No one will be home and it's not like there's anything flash at your house for anyone to break."

"Yeah, nah. I don't need the drama," I say. Again. "I'd better go, Levi's coming over soon and I want to finish my English essay before he gets here."

"Whatever." She sounds mad. "Sometimes you are such a loser." Then she hangs up.

...

I think about what Tiff said after the game yesterday, about how Maddy was spreading rumours that I was bulimic. I hate throwing up. I couldn't. I don't know why she wants people to think that about me when it's not true.

"If you ever want to hang out without her, let me know," she'd said.

Mum is going away with Chris this weekend and Maddy is obviously mad with me that I won't throw a party, but maybe I could see if Tiff wants to hang out on Saturday after the game while Levi is at his boxing class. I probably need to get some better friends.

I send Tiff a text.

* * *

Racquel calls me to set the table and I go downstairs. Kael helps. We're only having forks but he puts them round the wrong way while I fill our water glasses and put the jug in the middle of the table. Tonight we're having lentil and spinach curry, which tastes more like soup and needs some seasoning. If Mum was making curry, we'd have roti or poppadoms with mango pickle and raita, but Racquel doesn't even do rice.

Dad appears as we're sitting down, looking grumpy. He's been round at Mum's house.

"Does she think it's funny that loverboy made all that extra work for me?" He spoons curry into his bowl and grinds heaps of pepper on top. We don't have salt at their house. "We should have got a place with a bigger garden and no covenants about advertising. Then I wouldn't have to deal with that dickhead."

"Keith, language." Racquel frowns and looks to see if Kael heard him. He did. It looks like he's storing the word up for later. I kind of want him to say it. He's always copying me. Last week I got him to say 'wanker' over and over because it was cute.

"Well, you didn't see what that ... idiot did, did you! The bloody tree looked like a giant ... penis!"

It was mortifying actually. I was so glad Maddy wasn't there to see it. She would have told everyone at school. It's kind of good that Dad was so pissy and fixed it the same day because I don't think anyone saw. Imagine if Levi had walked past? Also, our house is right opposite the bus stop for school. We'd probably have been known as the 'penis house' for the rest of my life. I wouldn't even be able to finish my education and I'd have had to leave school and become a hermit.

Dad waves his fork at me. "How long has your mum been seeing that guy anyway?"

"I don't know. I think he was doing photos for her business or something." Mr Bacon probably felt sorry for Mum because she's old and lonely. He could have got someone much better. I guess she's a good cook so maybe she lured him in with that.

"So he's a photographer then?" Dad says.

I shrug. "He's a teacher at my school too."

"What?" Dad bangs his hand down on the table. "Well, that's bloody inappropriate, isn't it? What's the woman playing at?"

"Keith!"

"Bloody, bloody, bloody," Kael says.

"He's not *my* teacher."

"Still, it's not right."

"It's not anything to do with us," Racquel says. "Who cares what she does?"

"I do. I care about the types of people my children are around. And what kind of man messes with another man's bushes? He should do his own bloody manscaping."

Racquel clears her throat. "I don't think that's the word you're looking for."

"Bloody wanker," Kael says, banging his hand on the table.

Moussaka

Beef filling:

1 onion, finely chopped

1 garlic clove, minced

500 g beef mince

400 g tomatoes

2 Tbsp tomato paste

½ cup beef stock

2 Tbsp chopped parsley

1 tsp white sugar

¼ tsp ground cinnamon

2 eggplants, cut into 5 mm slices

¼ cup olive oil

2 Tbsp grated Parmesan

½ cup grated cheddar

Cheese sauce:

75 g butter

¼ cup white flour

1 ½ cup milk

½ cup grated mozzarella

1 egg, lightly whisked

Method:

Cook onion and garlic until soft. Brown the mince and then add tomatoes, tomato paste, stock, parsley, sugar and cinnamon. Cover and simmer for 30 minutes.

Prepare the cheese sauce. Make a roux over low heat with the melted butter and flour, then whisk in the milk and stir until it creates a creamy sauce. Remove from heat and after 5 minutes add the cheese and egg.

Preheat the oven to 180°C.

Layer 1/3 of the aubergine slices into a greased lasagne dish and brush with oil. Cover with half the mince mixture, then more eggplant, the rest of the mince, and a top layer of eggplant. Pour the cheese sauce over it and top with Parmesan and cheddar.

Bake for 45 minutes until golden brown and bubbling hot.

Eleni

Barbara was a godsend. Within a week, Eleni wondered how she'd ever managed without her.

The first day Barbara was due, Savvas had grumbled when Eleni tidied up the mess he'd left in the lounge before she arrived, then disappeared early to work. Definitely a first.

He'd been showering Theo though, and Theo seemed much happier and didn't complain as much. It made Eleni think she should have insisted on it years ago. He'd been supervising Theo's breakfast and even cooked eggs for them both one morning. Eleni had needed to re-clean the kitchen once they'd both left the house, but it was a start at least.

On Theo's day off from his day programme, Barbara arrived as Savvas was leaving.

"Nice to see you doing your bit, buddy. I'll get you to run the mop over the kitchen floor during the week when you're not working. I'm sure you won't have a problem with that, will you?"

Savvas grunted. He looked a bit intimidated by Barbara, who was grinning with all her teeth bared, rather like a hungry crocodile.

"And if you'd give the bathroom a wipe down after Theo's shower, I'd very much appreciate it."

It didn't stop him from complaining about Barbara to Eleni, but Eleni noticed he still did what he was asked, as long as it was Barbara doing the asking. Whenever he slacked off, Barbara would leave a large sticky note and a reminder with a big smiley face stuck to whatever surface he hadn't adequately cleaned. It was hard for Eleni to not do things herself, but Barbara would remind her, when she caught Eleni picking up after Savvas, that he was perfectly capable of pushing a dishcloth around and wasn't so incapacitated that he couldn't put his shoes on the rack.

* * *

While Howard was away, Eleni had been going to his place to check everything was still in order and to have a quick clean. Eleni was so grateful he was keeping her on full salary during this time, so she'd pop in, collect the mail, run the vacuum and mop over, and make sure the dust hadn't gathered. Ben, Howard's younger son, had moved in the previous year and lived in the guest wing, but she left that part of the house alone.

Howard lived in one of the nicest suburbs in town, in a huge 1940s Tudor-style house, which he'd bought after his ladder-making business had taken off. The street was quiet and pretty, lined with oak trees. All of the properties had high, private fences, spacious lawns, many with swimming pools or tennis courts.

When she pulled up at the house, one of Howard's BMWs was in the driveway and Ben was standing beside it talking to a short, bearded man in a dark, badly fitting suit. They shook hands and the man climbed into the driver's seat and reversed down the driveway. Ben watched him leave, looking smugly pleased with himself.

Eleni got out of her car.

"Morning, Eleni." He had his hands in his pockets and was rocking back and forth on his heels. "You wouldn't believe what I got for Grandad's car."

"Does Howard know you've sold his car? Did he ask you to?"

"Would I sell it if he didn't? Not anything for you to worry about anyway, is it?" He smiled, but in a way that Eleni knew meant he was putting her in her place.

She followed him up the stairs to the front door.

Ben disappeared down the hallway to his quarters, and Eleni set about cleaning the kitchen. Despite being several decades younger than Savvas, Ben was no tidier and she was glad he had his own kitchenette. She gave everything a quick wipe down, mopped the floor and took the wilted flowers out of the vase on the bench, carrying them out to the back garden to put in the compost.

Howard's garden was his pride and joy. He and Eleni often worked alongside each other, pulling weeds and pruning the rose bushes in companionable silence. It was getting to be a lot of work for him now, but the area was stunning after so many years of tender loving care. The house was stunning too, but for Eleni, the garden was the nicest part.

She'd given Howard one of the rose bushes after Ruth died, a beautiful pale-pink bloom with hints of lemon. It was still flowering now, the last blooms almost finished, and she bent to take in its scent with a smile before she headed back inside and upstairs to Howard's bedroom. Well, Howard and Vanda's room now, she supposed.

It was a lovely room with original wood panelling and a small balcony with a view over the immaculate rose beds. When Ruth was still alive they'd turned the small office next door, originally a nursery, into an en suite, and then when she'd got sick they had installed an elevator, which was rather handy now that Howard couldn't manage the stairs so easily.

In the en suite, Eleni noticed the toilet bag she'd packed but which Howard had left behind was still sitting on the vanity. Eleni had called Flea to confess what she'd done. Flea had said she'd contact the ship, and that had eased her worries a little. However, when she unpacked the contents now, Eleni noticed the Viagra pills were not in the bag, and the worry hit her all over again. What if he had taken the Viagra but not his heart meds? How would the family feel that she'd been the one to get it for him if anything happened?

It wasn't something Eleni could tell his children about, as it was a personal matter. Howard was a dignified man and she was sure he wouldn't want them discussing his intimate life. She'd have to hope for the best, and that he and Vanda were so busy during the day they didn't have the energy for extensive love-making sessions at night.

* * *

Ben came into the hallway as Eleni was gathering her bag to leave. She wondered what he'd been doing on Howard's side of the house while Howard wasn't there and hoped he hadn't made any messes she'd need to clean up next time. He plucked the keys for Howard's Volvo from the hook on the console.

"Grandad won't mind if I borrow this for a bit. The old bugger shouldn't be driving anyway," he said. He gave her a wink and hoisted the backpack he'd been carrying onto his shoulder. By the time she'd locked up and was heading to her car, Ben was backing out of the garage.

* * *

She had plenty of time before she needed to be home, with Barbara there for Theo, so Eleni decided to stop off and buy her mother a gift. Cora loved pretty things and it would brighten her day. There was a small boutique that sold in-expensive and colourful scarves and she picked out one in beautiful mermaid blues. There was a dress hanging on a rack beside the counter that caught her eye and, on a whim, she tried it on. Eleni hadn't spent money on herself for so long and it was on sale, so she bought it, not feeling at all guilty, for a change, for doing something for herself.

. . .

Alan had mentioned that the kitchen was short-staffed and that it was lucky most of the residents didn't remember what they'd eaten the previous night or they would all be complaining about having stew so often. Eleni had taken to bringing in a few extra portions for the residents who did notice, and for Alan who loved her cooking. She'd take some moussaka in for them the next day when she dropped off the scarf.

. . .

Theo and Barbara were at the kitchen counter when Eleni arrived home, peeling vegetables for dinner. Barbara favoured plain cooking, but Eleni found she didn't mind if it meant she didn't have to do it herself. Savvas complained that Barbara's food gave him indigestion, but at least he appreciated Eleni's cooking more because of it.

"Look, Mum, I'm making dinner. Sit down and put your feet up," Theo said, and Eleni and Barbara both laughed.

"Theo's been a big help. He peeled all the potatoes himself and helped me mix the rissoles."

Eleni lifted the lid of the pot and looked in. The potatoes were flecked with patches of skin but he was getting much better.

"Good job, kamari mou, you're a big help for your mamá."

"We made some cupcakes too. Theo wanted to take them to his yaya tomorrow."

The cupcakes were garishly decorated with green icing and sprinkles. They looked nice and fluffy though, and all the residents would love them.

Remembering the recipe for the loukoumades she'd promised Alan, she went to get out her mother's battered old cookbook so that she could write it out perfectly for him.

Chocolate-dipped
Strawberries

....

Ingredients:

100 g dark chocolate, roughly chopped

400 g strawberries

30 g white or milk chocolate, roughly chopped (optional)

The quality of chocolate is important. The higher the quality of chocolate, the better these will taste. Baking chocolate works best.

Method:

Cut a strip of baking parchment and leave to one side. To melt the dark chocolate, fill a small pan with 2 cm water and bring to a simmer. Put the chocolate in a heatproof bowl and rest it on top of the pan, ensuring the bowl isn't touching the water. Stir the chocolate to gradually melt it.

Or, melt the chocolate in 20-second blasts in the microwave, stirring after each blast until melted. Put the melted chocolate in a small deep bowl.

Gently hold the strawberries by the leafy top and dip into the chocolate. Tap off any excess chocolate and put strawberries on the parchment to set. If you have any leftover chocolate, pour it onto another strip of parchment and leave it to set — it can be used again.

If you'd like to decorate the strawberries, melt the white or milk chocolate and drizzle it lightly over the fruit.

Tessa

The day of the awards ceremony, Tessa had dragged down a weekend bag from her wardrobe and realised she couldn't remember the last time she'd had a night in the city. Certainly not since she and Keith had split. She was quite excited. She'd bought herself a rather slinky nightie for the occasion and she packed it, thinking of the night ahead. Her phone rang.

"Hello, I was just thinking about you," she told Chris.

"Hey, I wanted to check what time I should come over. And should I wear a bow tie or a regular tie?"

"Regular, I think." She packed her heels in the bottom of the bag. "But why don't I swing by your place and pick you up?"

"Nah, it's all good. I need the exercise anyway, I'll bike over. Is four too late? Too early?"

"Four sounds good. I'll see you then."

The Bacon apartment was in a stylish block overlooking the water and had valet parking. They pulled up at the main doors and a young guy in a well-pressed suit opened her door, welcoming her and helping with the bags. Once they got inside, Chris directed her to the lifts and up to the fourth floor. There was a code for the door and then they were in. It was starkly minimalist, with large floor-to-ceiling windows that showcased the amazing view. There was a sleek galley kitchen, white leather couches and large pencil drawings on the walls. The bedroom had a super king bed with a white cloud of a duvet and eight pillows. It was exorbitantly expensive looking. In the bathroom she found a spa bath and walk-in shower, gold taps and a bidet.

Something in her expression must have given away her thoughts, because Chris laughed.

"I know, it's a bit pretentious, but it's right next to the convention centre and it's free."

"No, it's lovely. Amazing. But it's not what I was expecting. Not very ... you, I guess?"

"No. Dad got it when we were kids. It was probably a place for him to have affairs, to be honest. It's only one bedroom so we never stayed in it as kids." He took some long-stemmed flutes out of a cupboard. They looked like they might be Waterford crystal. "We all had some pretty good parties here when we were teenagers though, mostly unknown to Mum and Dad. Plus it's a super-comfy bed," he added with a wink. He opened the massive stainless steel fridge and took out a bottle of champagne and some chocolate-dipped strawberries on a platter.

"Who put those in there?" Tessa said, going over to take a glass from him.

"Flea was in town yesterday so she did it." He popped the cork and poured. "Congratulations Tessa, I'm so proud of you, win or not." They clinked glasses.

...

She couldn't believe it when she won.

They'd called her name and she was already clapping for whoever she'd assumed had beaten her. Then Chris was nudging her forward and she realised it was her. It was surreal. It was only an industry award, but it felt like she'd won an Oscar. She'd made a terrible, fumbling speech and then she had to pose for photos.

After far too many champagnes and a lovely but tiny meal, she and Chris headed back to the apartment where she kicked off her shoes and sighed with relief.

"I cannot believe I won," she said for the hundredth time. Chris grinned. He'd taken a few photos of her too, holding the gold pepper mill trophy and grinning like a woman possessed.

"You could put a sticker on all the product jars now," he told her, rummaging through the drawers.

"What are you looking for?" She took off her earrings and set them on the side table beside the sofa.

"A takeout menu. I'm starving. Do you want pizza or Chinese?"

"I shouldn't," Tessa said, but her stomach disagreed. "You know what, pizza would be amazing. Margherita, please."

It took ages to arrive. Chris had taken off his suit and was in his undies and a T-shirt when the concierge rang to say that the delivery guy was in the foyer and that someone would need to come down to collect it. Tessa went, barefoot and with her make-up off, looking far less glamorous than when they'd left earlier.

...

When she came back, Donald and Margot were at the front door arguing with Chris.

"Yes, but there's a booking process," he was saying. "I already booked it for tonight and if you'd checked you would have seen that. Can't you and Dad go to a hotel?"

"Hello," Tessa said clumsily, waving one hand while the other balanced the pizza. Chris's parents turned to look at her, taking her in.

"Goodness, hello. It's Vanda's daughter, isn't it?" Donald said finally.

"Is it?" Margot peered at her. "Wherever are your shoes, dear? Have you been mugged?"

"Turns out, Tessa has an apartment in the same building," Chris said quickly. "We met coming in, didn't we, Tessa. With Brady. He's here too. Flea is coming over so we thought we'd all share a pizza and get to know one another a bit better." He sounded completely panicked. Tessa didn't know what was going on until she remembered that Chris had said he hadn't told his family about separating from Leanne. They'd been going out for a while now though and she had assumed that he had at least come clean to his parents. Flea knew. Even her kids knew. It was a bit thorny, but surely he could have told his parents rather than come up with some flimsy reason they had been caught together. Now they would think he was having an affair. With her.

"Well, it's a bloody nuisance," Donald said, looking suspiciously at Chris. "We'll have to get a driver home, I suppose. I can't risk another DUI. Come on then, Margot."

...

After they left, Chris let her in and she set the pizza down on the counter, her appetite gone. "They still don't know?"

"I was going to tell them, Tessa, I swear. But I wanted to wait until Grandad got back and tell him first."

"Do you think that they believed all that rubbish about me having a place here? Why would you have booked it if we met in the foyer earlier?" Tessa realised she was furious with him. "They'll think you're having an affair with me."

"I'll clear it up. It's tricky."

"What's so tricky about it?"

"You don't understand. After I turned down the chance to run the family business, they were so disappointed in me.

Leanne too. They all see me as such a disappointment. They think I have no ambition and when I tell them my marriage failed too, it's going to make it worse."

"Right. But it's less disappointing to them to have a son who's cheating on his wife? So, what, I'm a dirty little secret? Someone you're too embarrassed to admit to being with?"

Chris sighed. "You know that's not it. But it's awkward. They only know you as Vanda's daughter. I was hoping to win Grandad round first. If he was okay with it, they'd have to be too. Once he saw how great you were …"

"I think maybe I should go home," Tessa decided, feeling close to tears.

"What? No." Chris tried to take her arm but she pulled away. "Come on, we've both had a lot to drink. Why don't we have something to eat and go to bed? Let's not spoil your big night. We can talk about this in the morning, yeah?" She couldn't drive, she realised, and she didn't know what to think. What he'd said rang true, but she felt like he'd let her down somehow. Like he was ashamed of her. That she wasn't good enough.

· · · ·

They went to bed. Tess left the nightie in her bag and wore a T-shirt instead. They lay in the unfamiliar room with the lights from the city as a backdrop and she was pretty sure they both pretended to be asleep.

Feijoa Chutney

....

Ingredients:

1 kg feijoas, peeled and diced

400 g Granny Smith apples, peeled and diced

300 g onions, peeled and chopped

50 g fresh ginger, peeled and finely grated

4 whole star anise

750 ml bottle cider vinegar

500 g soft brown sugar

1 tsp ground cardamom

Method:

Put the prepared feijoas, apples, onions and ginger into a heavy-based preserving pan or wide-based saucepan.

Pour 1/2 cup of water over it and add the star anise.

Cook over a low to medium heat for about 30 minutes, or until the fruit and onions are soft. Add the cider vinegar, brown sugar and cardamom. Stir and bring to the boil. Reduce heat and simmer gently for 1—1½ hours until chutney is thick. Stir occasionally during cooking to avoid the chutney catching on the bottom of the pan.

Pour into sterilised jars and seal. Allow to mature for a month to six weeks before eating. Great served with cheese and cold meats.

Tessa

The drive back the next morning was uncomfortable, to say the least. Tessa told Chris she needed to get home to make up a batch of feijoa chutney, which was only partly true, and they skipped the nice brunch they'd been planning. Instead, they grabbed a coffee and bacon and egg roll from the cafe next to the apartment block and ate in the car.

It started to rain on the way home and Tessa offered to drop Chris at his place, but instead he got her to let him out at the school, saying he needed to do a couple of things and that he'd Uber home. As she pulled away, she realised she had no idea where he even lived. In fact, she knew very little about him, apart from what he'd told her. For all she knew, he could still be living with Leanne. How many guys have spun a story like 'we're separated but we still live in the same house' that turns out to be 'my wife doesn't know we're separated and we share the same bed'?

Then again, he hadn't hidden her from Freddie, and surely

he wouldn't do that if he and Leanne were still together? Or was Freddie too young to know she was more than a friend? She didn't know what to think and she was still feeling dejected about the situation.

...

To make things worse, when Tessa stepped inside, there was a huge mess in the kitchen. It looked like Abigail had cooked breakfast and there were dishes that hadn't been put into the dishwasher strewn across the bench. A pot with burnt scrambled eggs was soaking in the sink and the milk hadn't been put away.

She took her bag upstairs, unpacked and took out the trophy. It was hard not to cry when she thought about how excited she'd felt the day before when she was packing to go. When she'd won the trophy and they'd walked back to the apartment, holding hands, Tessa had begun to think that this could be it. Chris could be the one. Up until then she'd enjoyed being with him and got butterflies whenever she saw him, even when she thought of him. But last night, with the commotion of the city around them, the wind and biting cold chilling her bare arms, Chris had taken off his jacket and put it around her and she'd thought, 'I think he's it for me'.

She hadn't meant to blurt out the 'I love you' the other day in the garden, and she and Chris hadn't talked about it, but she was feeling it. She hadn't meant it in that way at the time, but she knew it was true. But she had no idea how Chris really felt about her. Not *really*.

...

After she sorted the kitchen, she started on a batch of chutney. It would have to be stored for a few months until it was ready and she thought about turning Thomas's room into a storage area and office. She was using the garage at the moment but it would be nicer to have a room especially for her business. The garage wasn't internal, so it sucked in winter. Where would Thomas sleep if he needed to come home though?

The room filled with the smell of feijoas and Tessa wrote out a list of all the things she needed to get done for the week. Abigail's photo shoot was next weekend so she needed to have all her business stuff done by Thursday. Luckily this shoot was fairly local so there was no big drive. They were filming at a sports stadium. She hoped Abigail would enjoy it.

Loading a few pictures of her award win onto her Instagram page, she checked carefully to make sure they were right before she hit 'Share'.

She would do up Thomas's room, she decided, and maybe she could paint Abigail's too. It would be a good project for them to do together. She made a note to look for shelving and paint.

"Well, how did it go?" Sonya called out, opening the door

and poking her head in. "Oh, well, there's always next year, hun," she said when she saw Tessa's face.

"Actually, I won," Tessa said, trying to look more enthusiastic than she was feeling.

"What? Oh my goodness, Tessa, that's amazing." She gave Tessa a hug, then pulled back slightly. "Why aren't you more thrilled? Why aren't we cracking open champagne?"

"I am thrilled. It is amazing, it's just that Chris and I had a bit of a falling out last night."

Sonya frowned. "Do we need alcohol? Ice cream?"

They decided on a beer each and sat at the table while Tessa explained. Sonya listened carefully, saying nothing until Tessa finished, then put her bottle down carefully on the table and gave Tessa a long look.

"You're probably not going to want to hear this, but I think you might be more at fault here, hun."

"What? But he was the one hiding our relationship," Tessa said, feeling a little hurt that Sonya wasn't taking her side.

"Sure, but it wasn't long ago that you were the one insisting that you keep it quiet. You can't pick and choose when other people are comfortable to out themselves to family. Expecting him to do it then and there and then getting mad at him when he didn't is a bit unfair, to my mind." She reached over and gave Tessa's arm a reassuring rub. "I love you, Tessa, but in this case, I think maybe you've just jumped straight into flight mode the minute an issue has arisen. Maybe that's to do with your dad? Brady does it too, you know. Runs at the first hurdle. And since Keith, any time a relationship hits a hard patch, you fold. Relationships take more than that. You have to dig in when the going gets tough. Stay and fight."

Tessa was quiet for a long time. Sonya sat and sipped her beer and let her process.

After a while, Tessa got up to give the chutney a stir and then came back to the table. "Bloody hell, I think you're right."

"I always am," Sonya said with a laugh. "I tell Alofa that all the time."

* * *

Chris came by that afternoon as she was finishing up her final batch of chutney. He knocked at the door and came in looking sheepish.

"I need to grab my bike," he told her. "And I was hoping we could talk."

Tessa made them a coffee each and they sat in the lounge. It was getting cooler now, almost time for lighting the fire, if she had any wood. She made a mental note to get some and wondered if she and Chris would get a chance to sit in front of it.

"I promise you, I'll tell them," Chris said. "As soon as Grandad and Vanda get back from their honeymoon, I'll tell them all."

"Okay." Tessa set down her cup on the old wooden coffee table. "Look, I probably overreacted, and I get it, I didn't want the kids to know either, so I'm being a total hypocrite."

"No, not at all. And I'm sorry if you felt like I wasn't proud to be with you. I think you're amazing, Tessa. You're sexy and smart and funny and kind. I need to tell you. I ..."

"Mum, I got my licence!" Abigail yelled, running into the lounge waving a scrap of paper around. "I can drive. Can I take your car to ...?" She paused when she saw Chris. "Oh, hi, Mr Bacon. I didn't know *you'd* be here."

"Congratulations, Abigail." He stood and collected the coffee cups. "Actually, I'd better go, I have a class first thing."

Tessa wondered what it was he was about to say.

•••

It was a busy week and they hadn't seen each other. Chris had extra classes to relieve a teacher out sick, and several photography jobs. Tessa was busy with work and sorting out the rooms. It wasn't until Thursday when Abigail went to babysit that they finally got together. Chris came over to help her paint Abigail's room. She had decided to do it as a surprise and had picked a teal colour for the paint and a new duvet cover.

She already had groundsheets down and the bed pulled into the middle of the room when Chris arrived. Things were a little strained to start with, but they got going, carefully working around each other, her doing the cutting in and him with a roller. She'd missed him and kept watching him from the corner of her eye as he pushed the roller with his lovely defined arms. Several times she caught him watching her too, and the room seemed to be getting warmer.

Their arms brushed as they both reached for the paint tray and then somehow Tessa was up against the wall. Chris was kissing her and she was tugging at his top as he pulled down her pants and she stumbled around, trying to shake them over her legs, blue paint spilling across the groundsheet and getting everywhere.

· · ·

It took forever to clean up the mess, and then paint over all the blue handprints and the peachy bum mark on the wall.

· · ·

They had finished putting the room back together and it was almost eleven thirty when Tessa's phone rang. She looked at the screen.

"Oh, it's Mum," she said, hitting reply. "Hello. How's the honeymoon going?"

"Tessa, darling? Can you hear me? Oh honey, it's awful." The line was dreadful, Vanda's voice cutting in and out.

"Mum? Are you there? What's wrong?"

Vanda made a sound like a strangled sob, then took a slow breath.

"It's Howard, Tessa. He's dead."

Spanakopita

Ingredients:

- 3 Tbsp olive oil
- 1 large onion, chopped
- 1 bunch green onions, chopped
- 2 cloves garlic, minced
- 1 kg spinach, rinsed and chopped
- ½ cup chopped fresh parsley
- 1 cup crumbled feta cheese
- ½ cup ricotta cheese
- 2 large eggs, lightly beaten
- 8 sheets filo pastry
- ¼ cup olive oil, or as needed

Method:

Preheat the oven to 175°C. Lightly oil a 23 cm square baking pan.

Heat 3 tablespoons of olive oil in a large skillet over medium heat. Sauté chopped onion, green onions and garlic in the hot oil until soft and lightly browned, about 5 minutes.

Stir in spinach and parsley, and continue to sauté until spinach is limp, about 2 minutes. Remove from the heat and set aside to cool.

In another bowl, mix feta cheese, ricotta cheese and eggs in a medium bowl until well combined. Stir in the spinach mixture.

Lay one sheet of filo pastry in the prepared baking pan, and brush lightly with olive oil. Lay another sheet of filo on top and brush with olive oil. Repeat the process with two more sheets of filo. The sheets will overlap the pan.

Spread spinach and cheese mixture into the pan. Fold any overhanging pastry over the filling. Brush with oil.

Layer the remaining 4 sheets of filo, brushing each with oil. Tuck overhanging filo into the pan to seal the filling.

Bake until golden brown, 30–40 minutes.

Cut into squares and serve hot or cold.

Eleni

Donald rang while Eleni was in the middle of making spanakopita. She covered the filo with a damp tea towel before she answered.

"Eleni, Donald here." He coughed. "I've got some bad news, I'm afraid. Howard has died."

Eleni dropped the phone and had to fumble to pick it up. When she got it back to her ear, Donald was still talking "... you could pick out something nice for him, if you don't mind?"

"Howard is dead?" she whispered. She felt like she might be sick. Or faint. She sat down heavily in a dining chair, her legs shaking.

"Obviously that means you'll be out of a job," Donald said, "but we do appreciate all you've done for Dad, and if you wouldn't mind helping to pack up his things before you finish up, that would be most helpful. We'll pay you for your time and of course you'll get severance too."

"Was it his heart?" she asked, afraid to know the answer in case she was responsible.

"It's all a bit unclear, but I'd imagine so. All I know is Vanda is going to be back in a few days with his body and the funeral will be next Tuesday." He coughed again. "I have to rush, Eleni, but if you could pick the suit? Maybe his gold cufflinks too — the ones with the ladders? I'll text you the details."

He hung up and Eleni sat in the chair and cried.

...

She was still there when Savvas arrived home.

"What's going on? Why is dinner not ready?" he grumbled.

"Howard died," Eleni told him.

"What? The old bloke? Well, at least it wasn't your fault, was it? What will you do for work now?"

Eleni looked up at her husband, standing in her kitchen, worrying about her job when she'd lost dear old Howard. She felt white-hot rage in her blood. She'd forgotten to get Theo, she realised, looking at the time. She'd have to go now and she'd still be late.

"When I get back," she said, "I want you gone."

Savvas gave a startled laugh. "What are you talking about, you crazy woman?"

"I want you to move out," she said, grabbing her keys. "I've had enough. I want a divorce. Pack some things and get out."

"Get out of my own house? You must be joking." He laughed again, but he sounded more unsure now.

"It's my house too, and unless you want to stay here with Theo, I suggest you go." She headed towards the door.

"Where am I supposed to go?"

"Your mother's? I don't know, Savvas. All I know is, I don't want to see your face when I get home."

She cried all the way to Theo's centre and then she cried some more when Theo told her he'd learnt how to use the bus that day.

"Are you sad, Mum?" he asked as they drove home.

"No, honey, I'm very proud of you."

"I'm proud of you too, Mum," he said. He was only parroting her, but it made Eleni cry even more.

* * *

She chose Howard's navy Ralph Lauren suit with a pale-grey shirt and navy and white tie. The cufflinks weren't where they should have been. Eleni had seen them a few weeks ago, so she knew Howard hadn't taken them on the cruise. The leather valet box had all his tie pins, cufflinks and watches, and now she noticed that his Patek Philippe watch was missing. That had been a retirement gift from Donald, and Howard never wore it, claiming it was 'too flashy'.

What else was missing? she wondered. A horrible thought crept in. What if they thought she had taken them?

* * *

Her nerves were raw and she felt as if she was going to have a heart attack too as she waited for someone to let her into the dementia unit.

The office had called to say her mother had been having some incontinence issues but was refusing to wear an adult diaper. The last thing Eleni wanted to deal with was this, but there was no one else. She was so stressed over the thought of Howard's death and the missing cufflinks and watch, and she was worried that Theo would notice soon that she was sleeping in the spare room. Savvas was still living in the house, though they barely spoke and he spent most of his time out in the shed. Now she had to talk to her mother about nappies. She felt like she was cracking into tiny fragments.

Cora was in the garden trying unsuccessfully to unlatch the security gate when Eleni found her. When she saw Eleni, she looked pleased, heading back into the home and down to her room where she went to her small wardrobe and pulled out her suitcase.

"Is it time to go?" she asked Eleni hopefully. "Now you have your fancy new house, I can come home, can't I?"

Eleni held back tears. She hated when her mother begged to come home and she felt so guilty for not having her there.

"No, Mamá, you live here now, remember? Where you're safe."

"But you have a big, fancy house now," Cora said, picking up her handbag and looking around for something.

"I just have *my* house, there's no big fancy house," Eleni said. Her mother ignored her, going into the bathroom and picking up her toothbrush. She took the pack of adult diapers off the shelf, turning them over and then putting them back.

"I told you he would look after you," she said. "He's a good man."

"Who is, Mamá?" Eleni asked, sinking down onto the bed wearily. "Do you mean Savvas?"

Her mother looked up from her dressing table, a photo of her mother in a frame in her hand. She looked at Eleni for a long time, then put the frame down.

"Get out of here," she said. "I don't know you. Why are you in my room?"

Eleni stood up slowly and edged carefully past her mother, her hands out.

"Okay, I'm sorry." She headed down the hall to the staffroom.

...

"Hello, Eleni, nice to see you again." Alan pulled open the door for her, the cloying smell of scrambled eggs thick in the air. He gave her a long look and then touched her gently on the arm. "Are you okay, love? What's wrong?"

Eleni burst into tears, folding herself into his chest. His arms went around her, holding her up as he stroked her back with a firm, warm palm.

"It's okay, it's all right, let it out. Life is a lot sometimes," he said. "Everything is going to be alright."

Abigail

I was so crapping it about the modelling shoot but it's awesome. It's at a sports stadium and there's twelve of us modelling and they're not all skinny Cara Delevingne-looking chicks. There's a tiny Asian girl called Mae who is a total sweetie, a black guy with dreads who does javelin, someone with blue hair that has the dopest tattoo on their shoulder of a dragon, and a chick with a blade for her right leg, who is so pretty she reminds me of Gigi Hadid. We're in the clubhouse changing rooms doing make-up with, like, professional make-up artists and there's a coffee station and sports drinks and a whole table of catering and everyone is really nice.

"You have fantastic skin," Pat tells me. They are the make-up person and Tony is on my hair. My eyes look so good. I'm trying to remember what to do to make them look like this all the time.

When we got here, Flea came over and hugged me. And

Mr Bacon's ex-wife and kid are here. His son is called Freddie and he's doing some photos too. He's funny. He was all excited to talk to Mum and he told us that since Howard has died, his mum says they are getting all Howard's money now. His mum was *so* embarrassed.

Mum still has bits of blue paint in her hair from when she and Mr Bacon painted my room. It's pretty cool now. I took the drawers out of Thomas's room too and Tiff and I are going to paint them. We've been watching YouTube videos for ideas. And Levi gave me flowers for getting my licence, which was so sweet.

We're staying the night in town while we shoot, which is cool, even if I have to share a room with Mum. We haven't checked in yet so I hope it's flash.

Mum has been kind of cool about everything. She said it's nice just us girls having time together and we're going to a proper Italian restaurant for dinner tonight. We both decided 'fuck it' to the carbs, except Mum said 'fudge it', and we're going to have pasta and we might get some shopping in too. Mum's finally got tired of her boring old clothes and wants to update her wardrobe or something, I guess. I can probably talk her into buying me some new trainers. I'm getting to keep some awesome stuff from the photo shoot too. I think I might change my whole image and go for a more sporty look.

I take a selfie and send it to Levi and Maddy and Tiff when I'm all done getting made up.

Levi sends me back 'CHUR U LOOK SO HOT' and a fire

emoji.

Tiff says 'Slay, so jealous! Have fun'.

Maddy doesn't reply.

...

We go outside where Antonia the camera chick is and some-one with light-reflecting shade things and I watch Mae pos-ing for a bit. They want me to start out wearing a tracksuit over a sports bra top. It's pretty cool. I'm going to be with another girl called Sienna who I've seen around at parties. I think she goes to the prep school.

"Hey, is your boyfriend Levi?" she asks and I nod.

"My girlfriend is mates with his mate Mathew. She said Levi is pretty cool."

...

He is cool. He's the best boyfriend. I'm totally in love with him. I think we might do it soon. We've been doing some other stuff. Levi said there's no rush. He hasn't done it yet either, so we want it to be special. Plus, his mum says she will 'cut it off' if she finds out he's 'using it', which cracks me up. He reckons she's only half joking.

She's probably worried about teenage pregnancy but Rac-quel has cured me of that. She had to do all these injections and stuff and now that she's pregnant, all she does is spew. And not only in the morning, like literally *all* the time. It's so gross. Yesterday she cried because she peed her pants while she was puking. Totally rank. I am not having kids until I'm at least thirty.

. . .

Flea comes over and gives me another side hug, careful not to ruin my make-up or hair that's up in a high pony.

"You guys look awesome," she says. "Abigail, have you lost weight?"

"Um, yeah, maybe," I say, feeling proud.

"Have you been sick? Make sure you keep healthy and fit. If you lose weight, you'll risk losing all that muscle definition you've worked hard for. Your make-up is perfect. Did they put waterproof mascara on for the pool bit later?"

I nod, feeling a bit confused. I thought I was looking better now I'm skinnier, but Levi said he thinks I'm nuts and I didn't need to lose any weight at all.

Sienna smiles at me. "I love how Felicity is all about strong bodies, not skinny bodies."

I look around. She's right. Everyone is athletic and healthy looking, not scrawny. They all look amazing, even if they're bigger.

When we get back after the first lot of photos, I help myself to a chicken wrap and a chia pudding cup.

I'm giving up on the diet.

Sour Lemon Curd

....

Ingredients:

2 eggs plus 2 egg yolks

165 g caster sugar (or other sweetener)

80 g chilled unsalted butter

zest and juice of 2 large lemons

Method:

Whisk whole eggs, yolks and caster sugar in a saucepan until smooth, then place the pan over a low heat. Add the butter, lemon zest and juice and whisk continuously until thickened. Strain through a sieve into a sterilised jar.

Lemon curd keeps, covered, in the fridge for 2 weeks.

Tessa

They were early to the stadium for the photo shoot at Abigail's insistence and Tessa was feeling a little frayed around the edges. She'd been up until well past midnight making lemon curd for a last-minute order, packing her bag and then on the phone to Vanda who was at the airport in Dubai where she had struck a paperwork problem and was in limbo, trying to get Howard's body home.

She and Chris had barely had the chance to talk. He was devastated and had been trying to sort out funeral things and juggle work commitments. The last thing she felt like doing was sitting in the stands at the stadium in the cold. She had her puffer jacket and a scarf plus a book in her bag as well as her laptop in case she got the chance to do some emails and invoicing, but her mind was all over the place with thoughts about Howard.

. . .

Flea had met them at the entrance and given them a hug.

"I'm so sorry about your grandad," Tessa said.

"Yeah, a bit of a shock," Flea said. "We should have been expecting him to go, he's old, and he hadn't been well, but he seemed so good at the wedding. How's your mum doing?"

"She's been stuck in Dubai, dealing with officials," Tessa said. "She's a bit in over her head, I think. But she should be getting on a flight about now, hopefully."

"Hello, Tessa!" someone yelled, and there was Freddie with his mother. He ran up, waving.

"Hello, lady," he said to Abigail. "I forgot your name."

"Abigail," she said with a grin. "Is your name Fred?"

"I'm Freddie Bacon," he told her. "Are you in the ad too? Aunty Flea says she is even going to pay me. But I won't need any money because now that Grandad Howard is dead, we're going to get all his money, aren't we, Mum?"

Leanne did an embarrassed, choked laugh and then there was an uncomfortable pause.

"Leanne, I believe you know Tessa?" Flea said, a bit coldly. She put a hand on Tessa's arm. "Sorry, I have to run. Catch up later?" Tessa nodded. "Come on then, guys, let's go see what colour dresses you all have to wear." She addresses this to Abigail and also Freddie, who protested loudly that he was wearing pants, not a dress, as they went across the field, Flea and Abigail grinning at each other.

"Shall we get a coffee?" Leanne asked. "There's something I wanted to talk to you about in any case."

...

Leanne was a fairly ordinary-looking woman, although fashionably dressed. Not tall, average sized, nondescript brown hair and pale-brown eyes. She wasn't gorgeous or hideous. Very normal. Freddie looked far more like his dad. Tessa realised she knew very little about her. Not even what she did for work or how she and Chris had met. She wondered what had made them start dating, or get married.

They waited in the line for hot drinks, talking about the shoot and the weather and then went to sit in the stands, under the covered area to get out of the wind. The cold blue plastic seats were unyielding and Tessa wished she had thought to bring a cushion with her.

"So, Tessa," Leanne said. "This is a bit unpleasant, but I'm going to get straight to the point." She gave Tessa a long stare. "I'm aware that you have a bit of a thing for my husband."

Tessa stared at Leanne, her mouth agape. She wasn't sure what to say. She wasn't sure what 'a bit of a thing' even meant. But to Tessa it implied that her feelings were one-sided. And 'husband'? Surely she meant to say 'ex'?

"What I'm asking, well, telling you, really, is that you need to back off," Leanne continued. "Chris and I are having counselling, and we're trying to work things out. We've been through a difficult patch, but we have a child, and we love each other and ..." She reached over as though she were going to give Tessa a pat on her knee, but then seemed to think better of it. "You need to stop mooning over him and let us get on with it. I don't know what you've heard, but we're not getting a divorce. So there's no hope for you and him, okay?"

"I don't ..." Tessa started.

"He's told me all about your little crush and, really, it's a bit embarrassing. I wanted to let you know, kindly, before you made any more of a fool of yourself. So please don't contact him again." Leanne got up abruptly and left, hopping quickly down the stands, giving Tessa no chance to respond.

Tessa sat there, her coffee going cold in her hand, and tried to get her thoughts together. She couldn't believe Chris had been fooling her all this time. Sleeping with her and acting like he and Leanne were long over. Making it seem like he wanted to be with her, when it had just been sex. And he'd been so blatant about it. In front of his sister, and Freddie. Kissing her in front of Freddie.

But not his parents. And only at her house.

He's been stringing Leanne along too, clearly. She obviously thought it was all one-sided. Chris had most likely told her that Tessa had hit on him or something. That he'd had to reject her over and over. Should she tell Leanne they'd had sex? But Leanne and Chris were staying together. Maybe it was best she didn't know. She looked over at Freddie, who was hopping along a row of chairs, arms outstretched, and she remembered how devastating it had been for her kids when she and Keith had split up. As much as she wanted to scream in Leanne's fakely concerned face that her husband had been cheating on her, she wouldn't do it. For Freddie.

What she did know was that she was done. Done with Chris Bacon and done with men.

She was so angry, but also so bloody sad. Her throat clogged with emotion. She was an idiot.

"Why are you crying?" Freddie had appeared beside her. She wiped at her damp eyes and cheeks.

"It's the wind," she managed to get out.

"Where did Mum go? I had to dig in the sand and this guy jumped right over me while they took our photo," he told her. "Oh, there she is. See ya."

Tessa watched him skip over to his mum. She could see Abigail down on the track, chatting to the photographer. She pulled out her phone and took some photos, then she opened up her messages.

'We are done, Chris. Don't contact me again,' she texted.

A few minutes later her phone rang. She ignored it. It rang again. Then it beeped with a text, then another. Tessa powered off her phone and put it in her pocket.

She should have packed tissues.

Death by Chocolate

· ·

For the cake:

cooking spray

4 cups flour

2 cups sugar

1 cup packed brown sugar

2 1/4 cups cocoa powder

3 tsp baking soda

3 tsp baking powder

pinch of salt

1 1/2 cups melted butter

6 large eggs, lightly beaten

2 1/2 cups strong black coffee

2 1/2 cups buttermilk

1 Tbsp pure vanilla extract

For the frosting:

3 cups butter, softened

7 1/2 cups icing sugar

2 1/4 cups cocoa powder

1 Tbsp pure vanilla extract

pinch of salt

3/4 cups heavy cream

4 cups chocolate chips

Method:

Preheat the oven to 175°C.

Line three 20 cm round cake pans with parchment and grease with cooking spray.

To make the cake, in a large bowl, whisk together flour, sugars, cocoa powder, baking soda, baking powder and salt. In another large bowl, whisk together melted butter, eggs, coffee, buttermilk and vanilla. Gradually whisk dry ingredients into wet ingredients until smooth.

Divide batter evenly among the cake pans. Bake until a toothpick inserted into the centre comes out clean, about 35 minutes. Let cool completely on wire racks before removing from pans.

To make the frosting, in a large bowl using

a hand mixer, beat butter, icing sugar, cocoa powder, vanilla and salt. Beat in heavy cream, adding more by the tablespoon until consistency is creamy but can hold peaks.

Frost cake between layers, and then cover the entire cake with frosting. Using your hands, cover the entire cake with 3 cups of chocolate chips, using more if needed.

In the microwave, melt remaining 1 cup chocolate chips, then drizzle the melted chocolate over the cake and serve.

BRINGING HOME THE BACON

Tessa

The funeral home car park was full so Tessa drove around the back and found a park on the grass beside Brady's truck. He had stayed with Vanda the night before and Tessa hadn't seen her yet.

Inside, classical music played and a large group of older people sat in the pews with rheumy eyes, dressed in their Sunday best. Vanda stood inside the doors, looking tanned but subdued in a black pantsuit. Tessa gave her a long hug, both of them unwilling to let go. Brady and Thomas were there, looking bulky and awkward as they handed out programmes.

"Where's all Howard's family?" Tessa asked. "Shouldn't they be doing that?"

"Some drama with Margot," Brady said. "Donald had to take her out back. And I haven't seen the others. Why isn't Chris with you?"

"Why would he be?" Vanda asked.

Flea arrived before she could answer, hugging Vanda and then staying with her to greet the incoming mourners. Tessa had kept away from her the rest of the weekend, not wanting to get into things while they were shooting the ad. She was a bit surprised that Flea seemed so offhand that her brother was cheating. Then again, she and Leanne didn't seem to be particularly close. It was going to be hard avoiding Flea, when Tessa was beginning to like her so much, but she was dreading the rest of the day, being around Chris.

* * *

Ben emerged from the bathrooms, hunched over with his shirt untucked from his dress pants and looking overly flushed.

"You all right, mate?" Brady asked him. "Dodgy stomach?"

Ben did a weird nod and hobbled down to the front pew where he carefully sat down on the right next to Leanne, Chris and Freddie who was chatting to a woman in the row behind them. It was Eleni, Tessa realised. Looking pallid, her eyes red rimmed. A man was next to her holding her hand. Chris looked up and she quickly looked away.

Abigail and Thomas found seats on the left at the front and she, Vanda and Brady went to join them. Donald and Margot emerged from a door at the side of the room and he led her to their seats. She had a blotchy rash all over her neck and she was clinging to Donald, sort of rubbing up against him like a cat. Donald was stony faced and pushed her down onto the seat with a muttered 'for God's sake, woman, pull yourself together'.

The coffin was already in place on the altar. It was a beautiful mahogany wood, topped with a spray of white roses and lilies interspersed with rosemary and pale-pink carnations. A recent photo of Howard sat on the top. It was from his wedding to Vanda.

The service was lovely, and afterwards, they sat and watched a montage of photos. There were images of a much younger Howard playing sports, then standing with a ladder outside his business, at his first and second marriage and then with his children and grandchildren. One was with Freddie, who piped up 'That's me!' making everyone smile except Eleni, who sobbed loudly the whole time.

Tessa sat, refusing to look over at Chris, and held Vanda's hand. Afterwards, they filed out to the tearooms.

"We're having dinner after this," Vanda said, blowing her nose. "Did Brady tell you?"

Tessa nodded. She hadn't wanted to go, but couldn't think of an excuse. "Now let's have a nice cup of tea and something to nibble on, shall we?" Her mother's voice wobbled, but she straightened her back and went into the crowd to mingle.

"What the hell is Margot doing?" Brady whispered, inclining his head over to the counter where a large chocolate cake stood next to a stack of plates and forks. Margot had dipped her finger into the icing and was trailing a line of chocolate ganache down her cleavage and licking her lips as she eyed up a gentleman next to her who was looking very uncomfortable.

"What the hell? Is she drunk again?" Tessa asked, looking around to see who else had noticed her behaviour. Flea must have because she strode over to her mother and pulled her aside with an apologetic smile at the guest and his wife.

"What is going on?" she hissed to Margot as they went past.

"Relax, they're only uppers, darling. Ben gave them to me. That man looked like Rod Stewart, don't you think? 'If you want my body, and you think I'm sexy ...'" Margot's singing was cut off by the closing of the bathroom doors.

* * *

"Tessa, can we talk?" Chris said.

Tessa's brain screamed 'No, I don't want to talk to you', but he had his hand on her arm and they were surrounded by people. To say no would cause a scene, and the last place she wanted to cause a scene was at his grandfather's funeral. Chris looked tired, as though he hadn't been sleeping well. He had dark circles under his eyes and his naturally olive complexion was pale.

"Actually, I want to talk to you too," she said. He led her over to a corner where there were two plush chairs situated beside an enormous pot plant, and gestured for her to sit down. She remained standing.

"You wouldn't want your wife to catch you talking to me,

hidden behind that plant," she said.

"What? Why? I don't know what you ..."

"She'd probably accuse me of throwing myself at you. And at Howard's funeral. How uncouth of me."

"Tessa, what are you talking about?" Chris scrubbed his hand over his chin. He looked oddly vulnerable. His grandfather had just died, but Tessa wouldn't let her sympathy overtake her anger.

"I don't appreciate that Leanne thinks this thing that we had was one-sided. And that you fooled me into thinking your marriage was over. Go back to your wife, Chris. If you're working on your marriage, then maybe you should be doing that." She turned and walked away, in what she hoped was a dignified manner. Brady was standing eating a club sandwich so she quickly made her way over to him before Chris could catch her up.

He took one look at her and handed her the serviette he was holding. She shook off a lone piece of lettuce that was clinging to it and dabbed her eyes, then quickly blew her nose before handing it back to him.

"Are you okay? You barely knew the old codger, only met him once. A bit over the top even for an old sap like you, isn't it?" He drew her into a hug and she was reluctant to pull out of his bear-like embrace.

"It's not Howard. I mean, it's sad and I feel bad for Mum. It's Chris, but I don't want to talk about it now."

There was a movement behind them and they turned to

see Ben, slinking along the edge of the room, still bent at the waist.

"That guy needs to find some antacids," Brady said as an elderly woman in a black dress and sensibly matching shoes approached Ben.

"Very sad news, Benjamin, you must know Howard was my favourite cousin," the woman said, dabbing at her eyes with a lace handkerchief.

"Yes, Aunt Doris, very sad."

"Stand up straight, young man, I don't know why you're hunched over like that. Your posture is atrocious, and it's extremely rude." She poked Ben in the stomach and he yelped and straightened.

"Holy crap!" Brady exclaimed.

"Wow," Tessa echoed. "That's some boner."

Aunt Doris gasped. "Oh my saints! And at dear Howard's funeral." She slapped Ben hard across the face. "Someone bring me a chair, I feel distinctly faint."

Everyone had turned in their direction. Ben was gaping like a fish. A red handprint was developing on his cheek. Using both hands he tried to cover a very obvious erection.

Flea hurried over to him. "What the hell, Ben? Not you too."

"I thought it was Ritalin," he hissed. "What do you mean not me too?"

"Mum. She's been acting like a rabbit in heat. She said you gave her some little blue pills. Can you please go and do something about that ... thing." She gave him a push in the direction of the bathrooms and Ben, hunched over again, scuttled off.

"Everyone, please, enjoy the refreshments," Flea called, and gradually the guests turned and went back to their cups of tea and sausage rolls, although there were quite a few whispered conversations.

"Who would have thought an old bird like Doris would pack such a wicked punch." Brady plucked another sandwich from the table. "I think I need a proper drink."

Bananas Flambé with Coconut Ice Cream

···

Ingredients:

3 Tbsp unsalted butter

1/4 cup granulated sugar

2 bananas, peeled and sliced 1 cm thick on the bias

30 ml Jamaican rum

Coconut ice cream (see below)

1/3 cup toasted unsweetened coconut

1 lime, cut into wedges (optional)

Method:

In a large sauté pan, melt butter over high heat. Sprinkle sugar evenly over butter and scatter banana slices over sugar in a single layer. Allow mixture to boil vigorously undisturbed until sugar melts and bananas caramelise on bottom.

Remove from heat and pour rum into the pan. Carefully light rum in pan, standing back to avoid flame, and allow flame to burn out, about 30 seconds.

Divide ice cream and bananas between four bowls, top with toasted coconut and a squeeze of lime juice, if using, and serve immediately.

Coconut Ice Cream

....

Ingredients:

1 1/2 cup full fat canned coconut milk

1/2 cup additional coconut milk, or milk of choice

1/3 cup sweetener of choice, such as sugar or pure maple syrup

1/8 tsp salt

1 1/2 tsp pure vanilla extract

Method:

Stir all ingredients together in a bowl. If you have an ice cream maker, simply transfer the mixture to your ice cream maker and churn according to the manufacturer's directions for your specific machine.

If you don't have an ice cream maker, you can
freeze the mixture in ice cube trays, then blend
the frozen ice cubes in a high-speed blender
such as a Vitamix.

Tessa

The restaurant was quiet. It was a Tuesday and they were the only ones there. Tessa sat as far from Chris as she could, at the other end of the table. Leanne was sitting next to him. She saw them deep in conversation, Leanne with her hand on his shoulder, and she looked away. Ben and Margot seemed to be somewhat recovered, both of them less red and blotchy, and drinking like fish. Eleni had joined them at the table, along with someone she introduced as Alan, and so had Doris and another woman, Annette, Howard's daughter who had flown over from Sydney.

Donald stood and raised his glass, clearing his throat dramatically.

"Thank you all for coming," he said. "I'd like you all to raise your glass to Dad. He was a wonderful father, grandfather and great-grandfather, and an astute businessman — his safety ladder will remain his legacy, and we will continue to honour him by producing it for many years to come. I'm sure he's up there with Mum now, looking down on us all and watching over us."

Freddie looked up at the ceiling and then tugged on Flea's sleeve.

"How did Grandpa get up on the roof?" he asked her.

The waitress came to deliver the first of their courses and then Vanda stood.

"Thank you to everyone who has spoken to me so kindly today. I want to say how exceedingly sad I am to have to come back from what was a wonderful trip, alone."

Ben gave a loud cough that sounded like he was saying 'bullshit'. Vanda ignored him. "Howard spoke of you all so often, he loved you all so much." She sipped her drink. "When he died, it was totally unexpected. We all knew he hadn't been well, but it was such a shock. I guess we all thought it would be his heart that got him in the end ..."

"It wasn't his heart?" Eleni said loudly at the end of the table. "But his pills? He left them behind and I thought ..."

"Oh, no, Eleni. After I got your message, I arranged for the ship's doctor to get a replacement script straightaway. No, his heart was fine. Did no one tell you how he died?"

Eleni shook her head, her hand over her own heart, eyes wide.

"I don't think any of us know exactly how he died, actually," Flea said.

"I'm sorry, I assumed Donald had told you." Vanda topped up her glass of water and took another sip. "We were on a shore excursion to a remote village. Howard saw one of his old original safety ladders propped up against a palm tree. He remarked that it was in excellent condition for its age and he hadn't seen that particular model in over thirty years and went over to inspect it. A coconut fell on him. Straight on his head. It was instant. They tell me he wouldn't have known what hit him."

Eleni made a choked noise almost like a laugh and then looked at Alan and smiled. It was a bit odd, Tessa thought.

"How handy for you," Ben muttered loudly.

Vanda looked over at him, giving him a long look. "Did you have something you wanted to say, Ben?" she asked softly.

"I just think it's interesting, don't you? How this is the third time you've been married, and the third time you've been widowed," Ben said in a rather slurred voice. "And now *all* his money will go to you, won't it?"

"What? No, it won't, will it?" Leanne asked Chris.

"Ben," Vanda said in a patient voice. "Let me explain something to you, if I may?" Ben huffed and signalled for another whisky from the waitress.

"Firstly, Howard and I had a prenuptial agreement. One that I asked for. I don't want Howard's money. I never did."

"Well, that's good, isn't it?" Leanne said. "Very sensible."

"Secondly, Howard knew what you were doing, Ben. He knew about the jewellery, swapping the gems for paste, about pawning off his silverware, and stealing his pills."

"Oh, good grief, that was Howard's Viagra, wasn't it?" Flea

pinched the bridge of her nose and sighed.

"The watch and the cufflinks," Eleni said. "You took them? And you sold his car?"

"What? I don't know what the hell you're talking about," Ben said, eyes darting around the room.

"Howard knew about the gambling and the addiction issues, Ben," Vanda continued. "He was hoping that mentioning the jewellery at the wedding would stop things, but all he wanted to do was help you. You need to get help."

"Ben," Chris said, "she's right. This has been going on too long. You need to go to rehab, mate."

Ben looked around the table, then put his head in his hands and wept softly. Vanda came around the table and put her arm around him.

"Will you try?" she asked him gently. "For Howard? It's what he would have wanted."

He nodded and then stood, pushing his chair back shakily before he hugged Vanda. "You're right. I need to get some help. I will. I promise. I'm so sorry, Vanda ..." The waitress had arrived with his drink and she stood there awkwardly. Ben took the glass from her and put it down on the table. "I'm going to leave. I need to go." Flea came around and helped him walk outside, her phone out to book an Uber for him.

Everyone sat looking at each other, not sure what to do. Vanda sat back down and dabbed at her eyes with her napkin. The wait staff came to clear the plates and they all sat in silence.

"Well, isn't that marvellous? Ben is going off to rehab," Margot said cheerfully. "I think we should all have a drink to celebrate, don't you?"

"Oh, for crying out loud," Chris said.

As they picked at their main courses, a waiter rolled out a trolley and started to set up a pan to flame the dessert. They all watched as he poured rum over sliced bananas and set it alight. Tessa couldn't help but think it was a rather inappropriate dish to have after a funeral. She tried not to think about how Howard had gone to be cremated after the service.

"Coconut ice cream?" a waiter asked Eleni, and she made that weird noise again. Eventually everyone had been served their desserts and they started to eat. It was very uncomfortable.

"It's good about the money though, at least, isn't it?" Leanne said, breaking the silence. "Do we know when the estate will go through?

"Will you shut up about the bloody money!" Chris yelled.

"Christopher, calm down," Donald said. "You're creating a scene and there's no need to speak to your wife like that."

"Abigail, would you mind taking Freddie to look at the fish?" Flea asked. Abigail got up, giving Tessa a puzzled look as she led Freddie over to a large tank by the windows.

"She's not my wife," Chris said.

Ginger Kisses

....

Ingredients:

125 g butter, softened

1/2 cup white sugar

2 eggs

1 cup flour

1 cup cornflour

3 tsp ground ginger

1 tsp baking powder

raspberry jam

icing sugar

Method:

Preheat the oven to 200°C. Grease or line a baking tray with baking paper.

Cream butter and sugar until light and fluffy. Add eggs one at a time, beating well after each addition.

Sift flour, cornflour, ground ginger and baking powder together. Mix into creamed mixture, stirring well.

Drop small spoonfuls onto the prepared baking trays. Bake for 8—10 minutes or until golden. Place on a wire rack to cool.

When cold, sandwich two kisses together with raspberry jam and dust with icing sugar.

Tessa

"What on earth are you talking about, sweetheart?" Leanne said to Chris, looking flustered. "It's the grief," she told the table. She was looking rather pale.

"Enough," Chris said. "This has gone on long enough." He looked over at Tessa, then his parents. "Leanne and I separated a while ago. I wanted to tell you all, but then Grandad wasn't well, and I wanted to tell him first, but the truth is, we've split up."

"But we're working on a reconciliation, aren't we, darling?" Leanne said, touching his arm. Chris pulled away and looked down at her, his eyes wild.

"What? Is that what you told Tessa? Oh for ..." He looked at Tessa. "Is that what she told you?"

"Why would she tell Tessa?" Vanda asked, confused.

"Because we've been seeing each other," Chris said. Margot gasped, which Tessa found oddly amusing since she'd practically caught them red-handed at the apartment.

"Don't be ridiculous," Leanne said. "This is all some big misunderstanding. Donald, Margot, this is rubbish. Chris and I are fine. Tessa is a bit infatuated, I mean, look at her. She's hardly Chris's type. She must be *much* older and also, she's quite … large. No offence to Vanda, but we know nothing about her family stock."

"What the hell is the matter with you?" Chris said. He looked over at Tessa, his face a mix of despair and something else. Love, Tessa thought. It was love. She knew Chris loved what was inside her, as well as her body. He'd done so much to show her that he thought she was beautiful, that he didn't see her as fat. She knew, in that moment, that Leanne had been lying.

"I'm so sorry, Tessa," Chris said.

"No, I am," she told him. "I'm an idiot. I should never have listened to her."

"Chris, please, think of Freddie," Leanne said.

"Shut up, Leanne," Flea said. "It's funny how you're suddenly so keen to sort things out now that you think Chris is going to be rich. This has nothing to do with Freddie. You weren't so supportive when he didn't want to go into the family business. What did you call him? A lowly teacher with no ambition, wasn't it?"

A waitress cleared her throat awkwardly and placed a tiered plate on the table. "Ginger kisses," she said. "Would anyone like coffee?"

"Hang on, wait. You and Chris?" Vanda said. "Why didn't

you tell me, Tessa?"

"Well, it was a little tricky, what with us sort of being related," Tessa said.

"Not any more," Thomas pointed out helpfully.

"Is it serious?" Vanda asked.

"It is,' Chris said, "I'm madly in love with her."

"It is," Tessa agreed. "I'm madly in love with him too." They sat looking at each other along the table, grinning like fools.

"Well, it looks like Tessa will be bringing home Mr Bacon," Brady said, laughing at his own joke.

Bacon-wrapped Dates

Ingredients:

16 dates

115 g goat's cheese

8 slices thin bacon, halved
toothpicks

Method:

Slice the dates lengthwise to create an opening and remove the pits.

Stuff in a small amount of cheese and wrap the date in a piece of bacon, securing with a toothpick.

These can be baked for 7 minutes each side in a hot oven, or shallow-fried, turning until all sides are cooked.

Place on a paper towel after cooking and let sit for 5 minutes before serving.

Eleni

Alan had been so kind to her. He'd comforted her, and reassured her that Howard's death was unlikely to be her fault. He'd even offered to go with her to the funeral, which was so considerate.

She had been so relieved to find out how Howard had died. She'd almost cheered when Vanda told her about the coconut. But it had made her realise that she no longer wanted to continue nursing. And then Alan had lined up a job for her.

...

She was working in the rest home kitchen now, under Lena, a large German woman with a shelf of a bosom and a laugh like a machine gun. Theo adored her, and when Eleni worked weekends, he would sit in the kitchen with them, hair net on, and laugh every time Lena did. Lena had mentioned to Eleni that there may even be a job for him doing dishes.

Savvas had refused to move out, so she had stayed in the spare room and planned to find somewhere else for her and Theo. She was surprisingly undaunted at the thought of leaving her house, realising that she didn't particularly like it. She just hoped Theo would cope with the change. But at least he could stay with Savvas occasionally and still have the familiar surroundings.

Savvas had begged Eleni to reconsider, but she knew they were better off apart. Barbara still helped them out, and something about her no-nonsense attitude had helped Eleni to grow a backbone for herself. She wanted more, she realised, than just being a good wife and mother. It was time to find herself.

Barbara had become a good friend to Eleni, and Theo loved her too. Eleni and Alan had also become friends, often going to the movies and for meals out. Sometimes she would go over to his small flat and she would teach him to cook some of her family recipes.

They were wrapping dates in bacon when he told her that he wanted more from her than friendship.

"I'll wait until you're ready," he said. "And if you're not, then that's okay too. But I care about you, Eleni. I think we'd be good together."

So much for him being gay, she thought with a smile.

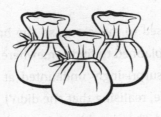

Money Bags

....

Ingredients:

large handful of fresh chives

250 g chicken breast fillet, chopped

1 clove garlic, crushed

2 tsp lemongrass paste

2 pieces of ginger, peeled and finely grated

1 tsp fish sauce

1 Tbsp crushed peanuts

1 Tbsp finely chopped coriander

16 gow gee wrappers

vegetable oil, to deep-fry

sweet chilli sauce, to serve

RECIPE

Method:

Place the chives in a heatproof bowl. Cover with boiling water, stand for 1 minute or until soft. Drain and refresh under cold water.

Line a baking tray with baking paper. Combine chicken, garlic, lemongrass, ginger and fish sauce in a food processor and process until almost smooth. Transfer to a glass bowl. Add peanuts and coriander and stir until combined.

For each dumpling, place a wrapper on a flat surface. Top with a heaped teaspoon of the chicken mixture. Brush the edge with water. Bring the wrapper edges up to enclose filling. Pinch to seal. Tie with a chive to secure. Trim ends of chive. Transfer to the prepared tray. Cover with a clean damp tea towel.

Heat oil in a large heavy-based saucepan over moderate heat (oil is ready when a cube of bread crisps quickly without absorbing oil). Deep-fry the dumplings, in batches, for 3 minutes or until golden and cooked. Using a slotted spoon, transfer to paper towels. Serve with sweet chilli sauce.

Tessa

Six months later

"Well, that was a shit show," Chris announced with a grin when he got to Tessa's. She was making sweet chilli sauce for her money bags and he was going to take some photos for her Insta page before they ate them.

"What happened?" she said, dipping a spoon into the pot and tasting it. Chris had been to a family meeting with the solicitor to discuss Howard's will.

"First off, the usual. The business to Dad, the bulk of the money to Annette with the rest split between the grand-kids, a donation to charity. Nothing unexpected. Except the cars were supposed to be sold and Ben already did that, the prick." He laughed, pinching a money bag and taking a bite. "But then, the big drama. Margot is livid."

Tessa swatted his arm half-heartedly and moved the plate out of his reach. "Photos first, remember? What drama?"

"The house," Chris said with a dramatic pause. "He's gone

and left it to Eleni."

"Wow, seriously?"

"Yep. Lock, stock and barrel. It's worth millions, so Mum and Dad are furious. Leanne would be spitting if she was still in the picture. I think she used to see herself living there." He laughed again.

"You don't care?"

"Nah. It would have had to be sold if he'd left it to the three grandkids. None of us could afford to live in it and pay the others out. Eleni is practically family. She's been around all our lives."

Tessa had only been to the house once, and it was beautiful. It was nice to think of Eleni living in it, and taking care of it.

Chris took the lens off his camera. "You know, I think the old bloke knew exactly what he was doing, leaving it to her. I'm happy for her. I might use some of my cash to buy a car though."

"The limo for Freddie?" Tessa said with a grin.

"Yeah, nah," he laughed. "I might get a little electric one, I think."

He got his camera sorted and snapped some shots of the dumplings and sauce. "Anyway, sorry if that was disappointing."

Tessa paused from biting into a money bag and looked at him in query. "What do you mean?"

"I didn't come home a rich man," he said. "So there's no

moving into the mansion for us."

Tessa gave him a long look. He really didn't care about money, or have any ambition to do anything except live a happy life. She loved that about him. He was content. It was nice to be with someone who just appreciated being with her and sharing their lives.

"Well, then, perhaps you'd better move in here?" she said.

He looked up at her, his eyes assessing. "Really?"

"Yeah, really. Abigail is off to uni soon, so Freddie could stay in her room when he comes over. And it's close to the school for you to bike. I like your company rather a lot. Love it, even. And I might get lonely. It makes sense." She dipped her finger into the chilli sauce and licked it.

"I love you too," he said, clicking a photo of her and then putting the camera on the bench. "Now quit doing that or we'll end up with a repeat of the cream puffs."

EPILOGUE

Abigail

It's a nice day, even though it's not quite summer. The garden looks really pretty. All the roses are cool. I've been on uni holidays for a few weeks now and I guess I'm lucky with the modelling stuff that I don't have to worry too much about getting a job over the summer break. Unlike Levi who is working in a fish and chip shop and always smells a bit like stale oil after he's worked a shift. It's a bit gross, if I'm honest. Still, he puts up with me smelling like chlorine all the time, I guess.

Maddy gave up water polo when we finished school last year. Said she was too busy. I saw her out one night and she was off her face. She called the next day but I was out with Kael and he was having a meltdown. He's not coping so well with the birth of Clove. Neither is Racquel, I don't think. I'm kind of glad to be away most of the year now, if I'm honest.

Mum's dress is actually beautiful. She looks quite nice and super happy. Everyone sort of weirdly matches, even though there was no dress code. The guys are all in dress pants and short-sleeve shirts and the women in summer dresses. Well, except for Margot, who's wearing some hideous black and yellow number. She kind of looks like a hornet. All she's done all day is complain about the lack of alcohol, even though we had champagne for toasts. Ben says he's fine if we drink without him, but it feels a bit mean to go too hard. In any case, Brady has a new girlfriend who I swear is too young for alcohol, even though he says she's almost thirty. Flea has a date too. It's Tony the hairdresser.

Levi takes the photos, which is really cool because he can put them in his portfolio. Chris gives him some other work sometimes too, when he has too many jobs on. Levi says he has given him heaps of good advice on photography stuff.

I ask Gran if it's weird having the wedding at Howard's old house, but she thinks it's lovely. Eleni has kept it pretty much the same, according to Chris. She has a kid called Theo who lives with her who has, like, autism or something. He's a crack-up. He makes me go and look at his pet turtle the minute I walk in. It's called Shelly. It's kind of stinky though.

Eleni has a friend called Barbara who lives in the separate wing of the house and she is kind of like a caregiver to Theo. She's pretty cool with some funny stories. She tells me that she was arrested once for possession of a class A drug. It was magic mushrooms and she'd picked them to make a risotto. She didn't even know they were the psychedelic ones. They let her off in the end but she said she was more annoyed that she never got to try them.

Eleni made Mum's bouquet and she and her friend Alan made most of the food too. Except Mum made the cake. Only it's not even a cake, which is weird. It's cream puffs, and when she brings them out, stacked up in a big tower with chocolate sauce, she's grinning and Chris just starts to crack up. I have no idea why. I think it was some sort of inside joke.

Recipe index

RECIPE INDEX

Printed in the USA
CPSIA information can be obtained
at www.ICGtesting.com
LVHW031213080624
782670LV00014B/811